Subcutaneous Stories

A collection of stories that aim to burrow under the skin and whisper sweet nothings to the unsettled soul.

David Holtek

CreativeDisease.com

david.holtek@gmail.com

Copyright © 2017 David Holtek

All rights reserved.

ISBN-13: 978-1979470544

ISBN-10: 1979470545

:

I began writing these stories a few years after I moved from the USA to the UK. Some came quickly, others had a long gestation period. The effects of such new surroundings has undoubtedly influenced my writing, but for the most part, my American sensibilities dominate in both theme and location. A few of the more recent stories reflect the fact that I've now been in England for more than ten years. Daily train journeys and the hard-to-encapsulate peculiarities of British life are gradually colouring my writing, so the occasional Briticism may appear. I hope both Americans and Brits forgive me for this. For the Yanks, to whom it may sound affected and to the Brits, to whom I probably just sound confused. Other international readers likely won't give a toss.

There is a sort of unsettledness that comes from being an ex-pat. Neither here nor there. In and out. It's a fine springboard for fiction. Stay unsettled.

I'd like to thank my front-line readers, Daniel, Ingrid and Marilyn for their indulgence and (occasional) brutal honesty. I owe much to David Rutland; his editorial and linguistic assistance has been invaluable, and our ongoing conversations continue to be a robust testing ground of ideas.

I dedicate this book to my wife Priya, who lovingly tolerates it when I inhabit characters and often speak gibberish. Because of her, I have a wonderful environment from which I can spring forth and jab my pen towards the murky depths.

CONTENTS

Meniscus	1
Just (the Jacket)	17
The Tarnished Heart	47
Inter-Narrative One	69
Crossed Wires	73
Muffler	83
Artist by Other Name	143
A Recording	151
The Wanderer	157
Horse Lion Encephalograph	163
Inter-Narrative Two	171
Cemetery Stories	175
The Message	193
Threshold	205
Café Compromised	223

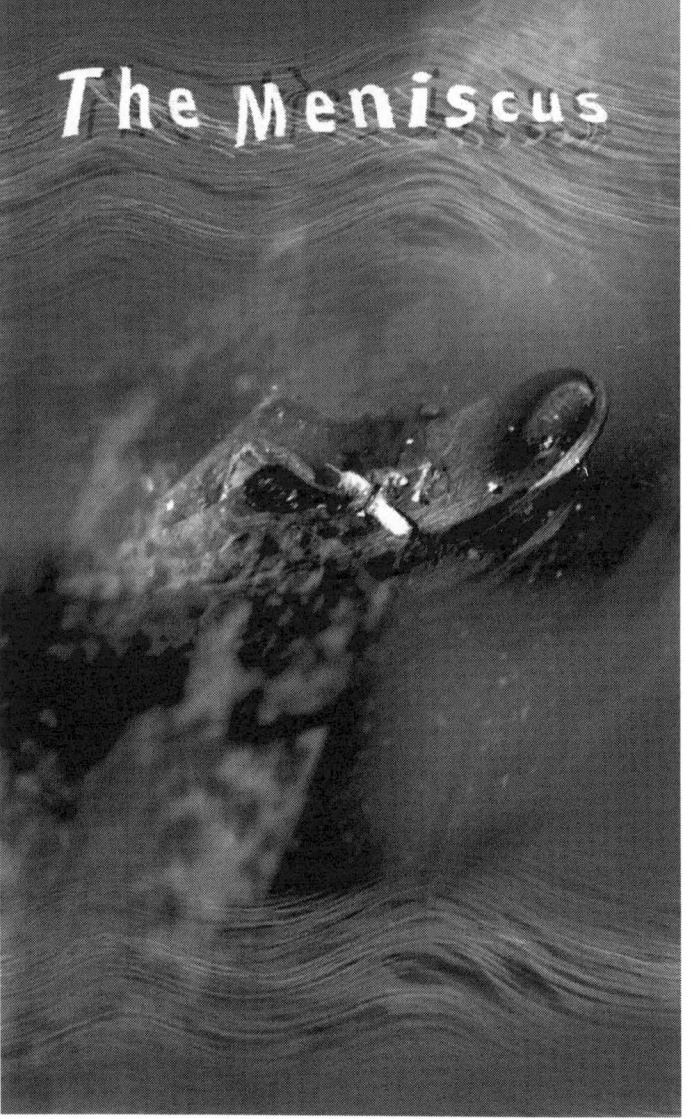

The Meniscus

The Meniscus

"You can't come out. You can't come out until you bring something up!"

The puzzled look on my fellow captive's face let me know that I had, for a moment at least, distracted him from our predicament. Normally, those words remained safely in my head, and I would only think of them at certain times. On occasion, I'd use them in a humorous way to lighten my mood. I've never liked shopping and have walked out of crowded stores empty-handed even if I really needed some item. If the item happened to be food and an empty pantry awaited me at home I might admonish myself with, "You can't come out until you bring something up". In this case, we might be talking about a can of beans.

Even though I wished I never heard them, I carried those words around anyway. Along the way, I decided to use them to my advantage rather than letting them weigh me down. True to my cause, I took their negative connotation and forged it into an imperative. If a friendship turned bad or a gal broke my heart, I was required to mentally or spiritually salvage something out of it - to bring something useful up from the murky depths of despair, if you will.

Of course, I never foresaw the day when the words

would feel so horrifically imminent again. As I stared at my trembling companion, trying his best to push himself further and further into the corner, I knew I should have come up with something more pleasant to say, but these were the only words my mouth allowed me to speak.

The old quarry, a part of which had turned into a large pond, was hidden in a valley surrounded by three hills. The story went that the ground there had become too unstable. I recall getting spooked as a kid when I heard speculation about huge caves being discovered below. No one seemed to know whether it was years of rain and run-off that filled the pond or if maybe water from below had burst through to quickly fill the void. If it was water from the depths of the earth, what hideous creatures might have come up with it?

The only reasonable approach to the pond was a path that looked like it had accommodated an occasional vehicle many years ago. If you faced the pond and looked up at the hill to the right, you could still make out a break in the overgrowth where an old service road once allowed access to the site. The road had long ceased to be passable. On a few occasions, I overheard my Dad drinking with one of his buddies talking about how some of them used to drive around the old, bendy road that hugged the hill. It was then that I also first heard the rumors - spooky tales of how in days gone by at least one or two cars had careened down the hill and crashed into the pitch-black waters of the pond. Nobody seemed to be able to verify it or know if the cars (and bodies) had been recovered. It was as close to an urban legend that our town had.

When you're a restless ten-year-old and it's a scorching August day, it's a lot easier to push such things out of your mind. My friend Billy and I would sneak off and go swim at least a few times every summer. I'd pretend I was an explorer in deepest, darkest Africa when we'd trudge through the tall weeds and push our bikes into the clearing in front of the big pond.

I always felt braver with my bike at hand. Even when I was just pushing it, my bike was my escape vehicle. At a moment's notice I could jump on it and be gone. I cherished it like the brother I never had. We didn't have much money, and that bike replaced a rickety old hand-me-down from a cousin. My new, flame red one with the banana seat and chopper-style bars was my symbol and tool of freedom. To this day, it is the only present I specifically remember. My dad was never one to horse around, so I expected nothing but a day of hard labor when he barked at me to go open the garage door. I tugged it open expecting him to tell me to grab a shovel or rake but there was only silence - silence and me standing there looking at that beautiful bike. The expected day of drudgery became a day of wild exhilaration as I pedaled off into the promised land of youth unchained.

That summer with that bike was as good as it gets. Every spot was a destination. Every destination a springboard for somewhere else. On the hottest of days, we'd ride and ride and then end up at the quarry. One particular day encapsulated and cemented my relationship with the pond, not to mention the world that lay beyond it.

You know, I've never talked about this, but after all these years it's crystal clear to me. I remember breaking through the brush and seeing the grape jelly-like surface of the pond. It was so still it almost looked like asphalt after the rain. No matter how hot it was, the water always felt ice cold as we'd tip toe in. The quarry was lined with medium and small sized stones that had grown slimy over the years. I'd plant each foot down carefully not wanting to slip or step on some broken glass that the local hoodlums might have thrown in. The slope was gradual for maybe four feet, and then it dropped off like the neck of a dirty glass funnel. In a way, it was good because it forced you to just get it over with and submerge yourself all the way down into the frigid water. I stood there with my feet still on the stones, maybe about thigh-deep, looking down into the water. The circular edge of the drop-off looked like a huge black eye staring up from the deep. As my heart raced I told myself it was just the cold water making me shiver.

With a good pal like Billy by my side, it made that first plunge easier, and a few seconds later we were both laughing and splashing around without a care. The bracing water made us feel alive and invigorated. The more we joked and laughed the less I thought about the fact that there was an abyss beneath my feet. I could feel nothing but ever increasing cold below me. The temperature gradient from my shoulders to my feet was stark. I was like a piece of litmus paper that went from red at one end to blue on the other as my head baked in the sun and my feet felt like bricks of ice.

Billy and I were dog paddling, and he asked me, "Do you think there are really crashed cars down there?"

I instantly moved a bit closer to where the gravel rose up and became visible at the edge of the black iris. "I dunno." I hoped my apparent disinterest would change the subject, but he kept on.

"How far down do you think they are? Do you think the bodies are still trapped inside?"

Such talk made me scared and nervous, but I didn't want to be a chicken and insist we get out. All I could do was join in. It felt like a way to cover up my fright by joking about it. Soon we were both letting our imaginations run wild. Thinking up the creepiest scenario felt like a way to defang reality.

Maybe there were old rusty cars down there. Joy riding teenagers drinking beer, taking the winding curve of the old access road too fast and losing control. With last-second looks of terror on their faces, the car crashes through the guardrail. Maybe they were from

The Meniscus

out of town, and for days no one knew they were missing. By the time folks started looking for them, no one would ever suspect that they were all at the bottom of the pond a county away.

I began to shiver as we hurriedly spoke those words to one another. My chattering teeth and vibrating vocal chords made me sound like I was speaking through the blades of a fan. With each addition to our wild speculations, the water below looked more and more ominous.

"What if we swam down there? Maybe we should take a deep, deep breath and dive down," Billy dared.

I looked down as I tread water. I could barely see my feet. They began to disappear into a layer seeded with green-black, spider web-like algae. I visualized myself lowering my head and diving down. By the time my arms reached to where my feet had been, I would already feel a ten degree drop in temperature. If I completely upended and then kicked a couple times, I would be in dark water with maybe just an anemic halo of sunlight left to identify the blackness ahead of me as being that much blacker. I'd be so frightened that I would kick hard and fast with one hand reaching into the unknown and then pulling back while the other forged ahead. How deep would I have to go to prove something? In the blinding depths, I might very well thrust my hand down and push it right into a rusty, jagged piece of metal. I would not be able to see that it was the remains of an automobile roof compromised by twenty years of being underwater. The numbness of the cold would mercifully lessen the pain of metal ripping my skin apart but not by much. If there was any way for the water to get even more opaque, the addition of crimson red swirls would do the trick. Perhaps the fish would smell the blood, and before long, I'd feel slimy things darting across my skin and face. The pain and the shock would finally come together and cause me to open my mouth and let out a gurgled, watery scream - just then an eel would dart into my mouth.

Maybe the car had come to rest on its side, and I'd blindly plunge my arm through an already smashed but still jagged window. My forearm would open like a freshly waxed zipper as I tried to pull it back too late. Perhaps my hand would penetrate the car enough to knock and dislodge a decayed passenger in the back seat. For years and years she had managed to stay there just barely held in place by a branch that had lodged itself inside as the car plunged down the hill. The force of my hand would be enough to set her free. As I'd try to get my feet back under me and begin a frantic swim for the surface, she would shoot out of the wreck like a torpedo. What was left of her hair all covered in slime would smack into my face and slither over my nose and mouth like rotten snakes. Thirty feet down, I'd dance a macabre ballet with a twenty-year-old corpse. Synchronized drowning. She'd want to come up - to be free of her equally rotten companions - I'd want her to stay down. If I managed to turn around in the water I might have a chance to kick her to pieces as I let out little girl screams that mercifully only the fish could hear. A few seconds after I'd break the surface, little bits of her would plop to the surface around me like fleshy fishing bobs. Still struggling to breathe, I'd realize that I had strands of her worm-like hair stuck in my mouth.

No. I decided that diving down with my friend was not a good idea.

On the last weekend of summer break, we took one final trip to the quarry. We were both filled with the potent mix of exhilaration and melancholy that always seemed to come at the very end of summer breaks. That last week of freedom becomes the most precious thing on earth. The air smells the sweetest. The grass is at its greenest. The butterflies in your stomach want to burst out and eat the flowers. If only it could be the week that never ends. When you're that young it's hard to truly value the fleeting nature of life, but by

The Meniscus

late August the figure of a scowling schoolmarm begins to breathe down your neck. When she bends down to grab you by the collar to drag you back to the tedium of the classroom, you catch a glimpse of the past three months reflected in her reading glasses. She yanks you forward so fast the summer spills out of your gut and sits forlorn on the ground. Your shadow manages to keep touching it until she's pulled you too far. You take one last look back at freedom and watch it turn to stone.

But it hadn't ended just yet. We still had it in our power to make it the best summer ever. We broke through the brush, dropped our bikes, shirts and shoes onto the gravel and ran up to the edge of the water. I stared at it. It stared at me. A ripple appeared, and I decided that the water had blinked. This is the summer that I shall master my fears.

We dove in, and I looked at the rocks as they swooped down towards the depths. I stayed underwater and focused on the rocky slope, following it with my eyes until it dissolved into a greenish black fog. It made me wonder if one could hug the side all the way down. Perhaps you could hold some weights, let yourself sink and gently bounce on and off the side. If you got short on breath before you reached the bottom, you could let go and scramble for the surface. Maybe next summer.

We ended up pretty far in, almost like we were both silently displaying our increasing bravery. We paddled around and talked a bit but mostly just enjoyed the peace and quiet. I remember turning my back to the shore and staring off towards the far end where the trees came right to the edge of the pond. I guess I heard Billy splashing, but I must have drifted off into a kind of eye-lock dream state. When I turned around he was grabbing his bike and pushing it as fast as he could into the brush. Before I could even holler at him, I saw the two boys emerging from the tall weeds to my right. I immediately knew who they were.

The Meniscus

Jamie, the skinny one with freckles, greeted me with, "What'cha doing, retard?"

"Swimming with his girlfriend is what it looks like," said fat Marvin.

I held my breath and tried my best to casually make towards the edge of the pond.

"Oh, no you don't!" said the wiry bundle of acne-tipped energy called Jamie.

"You can't come out. You can't come out until you bring something up!"

"C'mon guys, I gotta get home." I hoped my matter of fact manner would make them miraculously stop and back off. Instead they both picked up some of the rocks that led up to the water and tossed them at me. They weren't trying to hit me (yet) but were blocking my exit by sending a few salvos my way.

"Dive down and bring something up, and THEN you can come out," said fatty.

"Yeah, bring up a skull!"

"Or a titty!" exclaimed porky Marvin.

Jamie turned and looked at him. "How's he supposed to bring up a titty if they're all rotten, you idiot!"

"I dunno," sputtered the witless behemoth and they both laughed.

"C'mon guys, let me out. I'm getting tired."

For the first time, I felt panic begin to surge up in my throat. Two more rocks plopped into the water just in front of me. I looked down and watched them rapidly disappear into the ink. I imagined them sinking all the way down until they made a muffled thump against one of the crashed cars. Maybe one landed in just the right spot and dislodged the rotting teenager. Or maybe the shower of rocks angered them. I looked down and could half see what first looked like milk in the water ten feet below. The swirls and bubbles became faces – terrifying, angry, rotten faces coming up to drag down the bastard throwing rocks, but they'd get me instead. I would do. And they would pull

The Meniscus

me down with slimy appendages that felt like thorn-embedded tentacles. I would be sucked into the watery graveyard car and made to suffer forever as they filled my existence with rot and filth and gurgled shrieks for all eternity.

"I can't! I'll drown!" I didn't want to cry in front of them, but I was starting to believe that I might die that day. I guess the panic on my face and the fact that I was starting to thrash around scared them a bit. But they couldn't just relent. Jamie spotted my bike, grabbed it and carried it to the edge of the water.

"Then here, let's see if you can bring your stupid bicycle back up!"

In one twist and a heave he threw my bike through the air the way they do the hammer-throw in the Olympics. Time slowed as I watched it soar through the air sideways. It had a spin on it, and right before it crashed into the water, the handlebars and headlight faced me. The round, crystalline light gave me one last pleading look before the bike smacked the water.

"No!" I cried out as I swam towards it. My beloved red bike slapped hard against the surface. The splashing water ran down the front reflector like tears as it looked me right in the eye. "Goodbye old friend," I heard it say to me. "Our time together has been golden. I am so glad to have had you as my rider. Other boys might have ridden me for a week then stuffed me in the garage, but you befriended me and welcomed me into your life. The very things you saw and the paths you explored might not have happened without me, and I wouldn't have experienced them without you."

But I refused to accept this parting. By the time I reached for it, my bike was nearly submerged. I grabbed at the handlebar, but I was still swimming and my coordination was all messed-up. It felt cold and slippery and slid out of my grasp. I stopped and briefly assumed a dog-paddling position and looked down at the bike's quivering red frame. The surface

The Meniscus

motion of the waves caused by this crime and the encroaching ink-water from below made the frame undulate like a giant red snake. Then I saw it as wispy streams of blood coming up from below as the reflection of the sun off the water compromised my vision. Either way, the water was filled with grief.

Such horrible things ran through my mind. I dove into the water and reached for it. I grabbed the right handlebar with my left hand. My bike was halfway to vertical as the heavier back pulled it down. I yanked the load back towards the surface and tried to get my right hand on it, but I struggled to stay afloat. I barely kept hold of it as I broke my head above the surface and gasped for breath. I tried to turn my head to see how far from shore I was. As I frantically calculated the possibility of dragging it under water with one arm and swimming with the other, it slipped out of my grasp. I took the fastest and deepest breath of my life. Every single bittersweet smell of summer swept across the surface and filled my lungs. I plunged back under.

I had to completely turn in the water and kick to reach it. I stretched myself out and grabbed both handlebars. It was like we froze in time and space. The cold quiet of the deep became the stage of our sad, watery embrace. I tried to pull her towards me, but the weight of the world pulled her back. We were like two astronauts suspended in deep space, holding hands, knowing that if we let go we would drift apart forever, doomed to float alone through all space and time.

My body arched and my heels began to drift backwards until I felt like I might turn all the way round in the water. If only I had super strength I could pull my bike up as the front of me rotated around to face the surface. As water flowed up my nose, I'd let out an underwater war cry and propel my bike to the surface. It would break through the water and into the air. I would then complete my rotation and blast off out of the pond into the sky like a nuclear warhead launched from a submarine. With a fist pumped high,

The Meniscus

I'd meet my bike in mid-air and mount the seat. I'd bend my elbows, lean down and stick my head out towards the bullies through the chrome chopper handlebars. My face would look like a horrendous carving on the front of an ancient battle ship as I bared down on my enemies. They'd try to flee, but I'd run them over and ride off into the distance laughing and hollering.

Instead, I watched the handlebars growing dim before me. My clenched hands looked as though they were dissolving into blackness. It all felt so much heavier like the corpses from below had reached up to grab it and claim it as their own. Soon they would claim me.

I found out how difficult it is to cry underwater. When I took in a gulp of water as part of a sob, I let go. With my arms still outstretched, I began to float back to the surface. The black water devoured my bike. Swirling, dirty liquid obscured the front reflector. The last I saw of it was the curve of the once shiny metal handlebars where they rose to their greatest height before bending down to meet the grips. The handlebars were the tall, chopper kind, and I had pushed them forward so my arms had to be straight out to reach them. I thought it made me look cool and bad-ass to ride down the road that way.

At the last moment of visibility, the curve of the chrome tubes looked like closed eyelids. My bike had resigned itself and valiantly accepted its fate. With eyes closed, it began its future of darkness and loneliness, locked into the eternal meditation of the unknown deep.

I broke the surface gasping and coughing. Both bullies stood motionless staring at me. They looked more afraid than I was. I suppose once they realized I wasn't dead and they didn't have a murder to answer for, their relief showed itself in the form of running away in nervous laughter.

I dragged myself onto dry land unconcerned with

any broken glass, sharp sticks or mud. I just laid there for a while trying to catch my breath. I coughed up water and it mixed with my tears. I pictured my bike still sinking. I wondered if it knew that I had tried my best to save it. I wept like a baby. I would never have wished that fate on anyone, not even the bullies – to be left down there all alone in the dark with nothing to do ever again.

I took another long, rasping gasp of air and lifted myself off the ground and started the long walk home. I never replaced my bike. My old man eventually noticed it was gone. I lied and said it had been stolen. He wasn't happy with me, and I knew better than to ask for a new one. Somehow, I just drifted along until I was old enough to drive. I learned some things like welding at a trade school, but opportunities in my area were few, and I mostly worked dead-end jobs. By my late twenties, I knew I needed a change and a challenge, so I enlisted in the Services. I'm not sure why I chose the Navy. I guess it was so different from what I knew that it seemed the most adventurous option.

I have been able to see a few exotic parts of the world that I probably never would have otherwise. But it's beginning to seem like my challenging career may be short-lived. Perhaps, if we had more time, I would tell my frightened shipmate about my travels, instead he gets to hear the quarry story.

Right after I described gasping for breath upon crawling out of the lake to my reluctant companion, I found myself gasping for air again. Of course, it was an odd tale to tell someone who was struggling to come to terms with likely, impending doom. But let's face it, it was as much for me as it was for him. I guess one could say it was my life splashing before my eyes. I suppose it was a situation where we'd usually be expected to pray. Maybe he was the praying kind but was so scared that he forgot. His eyes were wide and his brow dripped with sweat even as it grew colder and colder. The moans and groans of stressed iron provided the perfect soundtrack for my macabre tale. When I finished telling the part where my bike finally and irretrievably slipped from my grasp, he let out a sob. I didn't know if it was for my bike or for himself, maybe both.

The nose of the sub pitched forward, and our descent quickened. At the very end, I felt a weird change in air pressure as if the crushing force of the depths had reached into us even before the hull gave way.

"Bring something up. You can't come out until you bring something up."

I no longer saw the scared recruit in front of me or anything at all really. It was as if the wet, black cottony filament of the old pond had found me once again and encased me. In those last glorious moments, the opacity began to turn clear, and I felt like I could see through the bottom of the world. Through the depths of the ocean below me, I saw the meniscus where the sea meets the bottom of that old, grape jelly pond. It was like a slippery boundary in the middle of an hourglass separating past and present. As our crippled steel tomb hurtled down, a blur emerged from the terrible blackness. The moment of recognition swelled my heart. My tear-filled eyes moistened the smile that illuminated my face like a glow fish in the murky night of the sub. My old friend had made an incredible journey and aimed to see to it that I didn't have to set off unaided.

The last, agonizing groan of the submarine let me know it was time. The widest grin of my life stretched across my face as I reached out my arms.

Like a pinpoint growing into an aura, the halo of the headlight warmed my face and filled my heart. Beaming at the wonders of existence, I opened my hands then gripped them tight and prepared to bring something back up and ride it all the way home.

The Meniscus

Just (the Jacket)

Just (the Jacket)

Once upon a time, in the streets of America, the thrift stores were the front lines in the battle for style. Back when polyester and bell-bottoms were threatening to assassinate taste in broad daylight, a fifth column appeared. Well, at least that's how some folks looked at it or perhaps how someone with a penchant for hyperbole might describe it. Prior to the metastasis of mass marketing, the used shops were one of the few places where weirdos could synthesize their own look even if it was from the skins and bones of the not-too-distant past. Feeling a bit out-of-time themselves, these punks, new and no wavers embraced the anachronistic, the futuristic and the plain old deviant. Time traveling in any direction as long as it's not this one. Nihilism as cultural scrubbing powder. Saying no instead of yes. Death to disco and 30-minute Prog songs. The new children of the night wished it all stripped away. Dancing with shifting aesthetics under a pale moonlight. The shopping malls, a relatively new phenomenon at the time, cast a foreboding shadow across this brief paradise. Clouds on the event horizon. They had Gap and Polo. We had Goodwill and St. Vincent de Paul. Slumming for the real versus spending on the fake. Verdant, vibrant and a bit mean,

Just (the Jacket)

this scene. For a while, sound and space were set free, but moments of sweet triumph eventually attract flies. The alternatives win some battles but always lose the war.

Silk shirts, denim, leather fringe and too much hair drove a small segment of society to desperate means. Buy it. Tear it. Swear at it. Put a safety pin through it - anything to show disrespect, a lack of deferral or to communicate the subversive ambitions of the wearer. This was war via garment. Screaming through fabric. But soon the club-footed men of Madison Avenue were stumbling upon the potential riches of consumerized teens. Give them jobs at the mall so they can come back on Saturday and spend their wages there. The marketeers sent agents out into the field. Little did that 17-year-old, social outcast girl know but as she flipped through the Brian Eno LPs at the shop, she was being stalked. A smartly dressed woman with a Fine Arts degree from NYC was sizing her up and jotting down notes. The cool chick's outfit would soon find its way to the racks. She had to sling burgers to get through school, while her taste in clothing made some exec's bank account swell. By the end of the 70s, you could smell it in the air. The banner was raised: we will seize your identifiers and wring them dry of content and sell the husks back to you at a profitable margin.

Punks tried to be so ugly that surely the mainstream would not follow. It's a short distance from the lapel to the soft flesh of the cheek, but the placement of the safety pin still matters. Once clothes took on the pain, the wearers reverted to softness. But this strange new world was never monolithic. The New Romantics forsook destruction and instead championed style. Glam. Europe between wars. Granddad's sport coat. Pointy shoes. The lot. Dressed to kill in the bowels of a dark club. These are the kinds of visions that might run through a person's head as they turn a corner and spot a thrift shop up ahead. Memories of similar forays

Just (the Jacket)

from the distant past playing out in their head. The perfect find that would be put to work that very weekend at a club. The exhilarating breath of the newly cool. The old hanging-around-and-being-seen scene. Cigarettes and cheap beer. Goth chicks and newly liberated queers. It felt like the dawn of something new and strange back then. Operation Recycle Everything was still a few years off.

But the vagaries of life have a way of predictably plowing under that which feels new. Commodification is always clumsily lumbering just a few steps behind. The marketeers make a grab. Winded and sweaty, they snatch originality by the collar and drag it into the shopping malls. As style is hauled up the escalators, it begins to dry out and ends up like a desiccated, discarded insect shell. A husk of what went before. It will soon go for $59.99. The former insect that wore that shed skin now scuttles off for greener pastures (or darker corners, whatever the case may be).

The death knell for cool thrift store finds was the advent of the "vintage shop". These vultures went around and picked the Goodwills clean, marked the wares up 300% and then anxiously awaited the invention of the hipster. As time would soon reveal, the age of post-post was just around the bend, and as all now know, nothing really matters in the afterglow of the great consumerist detonation. The nuclear chain reaction of worldwide marketing meant mutually assured destruction for the twin aberrancies of authenticity and uniqueness. Whatever remains of them exists in the background radiation of first causes. If their names are ever mentioned, it is with the self-dooming snark of the generation that managed for years to pretty up anti-intellectualism with irony. Unmediated individuality died not just from over-commoditization but from the suffocating stare of culture itself. Once culture became so tragically over-self-aware, any genuine sortie into self-realization was met with the jaundiced eye of the post-crowd. Jaded to

Just (the Jacket)

the point of seeing artifice around every corner, this era had a pop-culture reference for any aspiring deviation. Anything you do, you must have seen it on TV or read it in the comics and on blogs. A torn generation that smirks at life yet is compelled to overshare. This self-inflicted wound climaxed with the manifestation of the dreaded hipster - that Frankenstein monster born from a sea of victims drowned in the waves of over-consumption and focus groups. Mercifully, the grave marker came in the form of the selfie. Clothes didn't even matter much anymore. It had all become strained, like overcooked vegetables, down to the pure essence of narcissism. The facial expression that blotted out the sun. Exaggerated faces that confess, "I am past everything, and now all I can do is purse my lips."

After such a tirade as that, it's recommendable to take a deep breath and remember that none of this matters much. A grown man goes into a used clothing store simply to find bargains these days. Maybe pick up a couple long sleeve cotton shirts to wear when the living room needs painted. Might get lucky and find a pair of khakis that can be worn to work. It's horrible to have to spend real money on work clothes. In short, any bitterness towards the gruesome death of a fabulous bygone era is a fool's game. It puts one in league with the whining former sock-hoppers and (shudder) hippies still convinced that the 60s were the be all end all. No, it's best just to hurry along, get some shopping done and leave all this ramshackle cultural theory alone.

Fortunately, by the time the second-hand racks were bled dry, most of those from phase one had moved on and world-weariness became their fashion. Plenty of them held onto style by making the early finds last well beyond their intended shelf life. These early apostles of the alternative developed a kind of "weirdar" that could usually spot an old soul, art-type from fifty paces. Who knows, in later stages of

Just (the Jacket)

maturity one might have crossed paths with some 90s kid wearing the very same leather jacket that was scored from a thrift in '79, then finally relinquished in the late 80s. The matured former owner might be forgiven if he cracks a bit of a smirk at the kid who obviously thinks he's the coolest thing to ever wear that coat.

"You see those scuff marks there, kid? These, the ones along the ribs. That's where I slung my Stratocaster a thousand times!"

Back to the topic at hand. Within some of these old second-hand clothing stores, one could find outfits originally purchased before most folks had TVs. The best things on the racks were made to last, sewn with care. A human at the helm who was not a borderline slave handled and inspected them. Is it possible that love and attention permeated the fabric, whereas now all that potentially seeps in is 3rd World desperation and fear borne from a lack of fire exits? If objects can indeed contain spirit, then the garments of yesteryear must surely have a leg up on the artificial blends of today. Or perhaps today's clothes manufactured under duress take on some bit of spirit, only it's ugly spirit. Vibrations of despair get imprinted in the fabric and that's why so many people walk around in foul moods these days.

Of course the budget minded or outright down-and-out continue to frequent the second-hand shops, though it's more a matter of survival than fashion. Even now, an outrageously patterned sport coat from a distant era might make a surprise appearance on the rack. One might lift its sleeve and wonder whether it had been squirreled away in a closet by some former devotee of James White and the Contortions. It might not have seen the inside of a club since the late 80's. Perhaps if one reached into the inner breast pocket there may be a yellowed ticket stub from a Bush Tetra's show. Maybe the left sleeve had beer splashed on it at a thinly attended Section 25 concert

Just (the Jacket)

somewhere in the Midwest. The eight or ten people there who knew how lucky they were to be seeing the band nearly outnumbered by frat boys who had stumbled in looking for some brewskies.

Occasionally, some greying member of the old guard wanders into the shop and finds his eye drifting over to the coat racks, past the parkas and windbreakers over to the jackets and sport coats. The small section where a rare, true man of taste may browse with purpose. He'll leave others to shop the socks and used underwear pile. If he is to be tempted by anything, it is going to be style, class, uniqueness. And on one such occasion, the eyes scan past the field of black, grey and brown tweed in search of an odd man out. There it is. An outlier. A sapphire in the bland. Experience knows to keep expectations low as the thing is approached. The shoulder and sleeve reveal a patchwork of black, purple and green on a nebulous, dark background. Stark, yet somehow subtle. There in the rack of predictability is a Tom Waites sandwiched between schmucks in cheap wedding rentals. A pearl and swine. A slice of fine cheese compressed by Velveeta. The tweed to the right with elbow patches reeks of a failed professorship. A life spent in pursuit of the authoritative at a trade school. Whoever wore this was the token Humanities teacher at a two-year vocational college. He tried to teach Plato and the Renaissance to dudes anxious to get to welding class so they could repair their muffler AND get credit for it. Oh, seriously? Does it smell of pipe tobacco? Yes, it does. Yes, it does.

The old-school walking relic can nearly sense that he's standing in the same space as his 20-year-old self. Scanning fabric to spot a gem. Something catches the eye. The intrigue and sense of potential rings true. Sure, there may be no clubbing on the menu but the thrill of the hunt remains. Here was style sticking out of an assembly line of no class. If an inspector had noticed this one rolling down the conveyor belt she would have hit the emergency stop and called in a team to assess the situation. How could such a thing have happened? People would be questioned. The room full of tailors and seamstresses would all deny knowledge - as if it had simply manifested from out of the aether and into inventory. Back then, good taste and hand-crafting were still the order of the day, but this one was different. It was art ahead of its time. It was the Duchamp of sport coats.

Perhaps, that is how it happened, only instead of heading to the incinerator, the offending odd-lot found its way out to the back alley, and the humanitarian errand boy spotted a homeless guy and tossed it to him. Homeless guy sells it, so he can buy something useful instead. And just like that, our intriguing little jacket makes it out into the wild. Jacket of virgin birth and unknown origins. Orphan tossed out into the night. Run little jacket, run! Help style break free. Materialize on man just as you did in the factory. Become corporeal when he first turns to the reflective shop window and tips his hat and admires you, oh, smart jacket. Seek to adorn all men and thus produce the essence of second skin.

Our middle-aged fantasist in the thrift store shakes his head and laughs at such mental wanderings. It's just a jacket, but what a beauty it appears! Surely the lucky homeless recipient would have been tempted to keep it. Who knows, maybe if he had slid it on and stood tall his luck would have changed. He might have turned a corner and found a ten-dollar bill on the ground. Back then it might have been enough to get a cheap room and a shower for the night. The next day he ventures out wearing the coat and sees a "help wanted" sign in a window. Five years later he's made his way up the ladder. In ten years he starts a company that will change the future of technology.

There we go again. It wouldn't have been like that at all. The hobo would have passed it on in exchange for booze money as soon as possible. And sure enough,

Just (the Jacket)

the next owner was no owner at all. Let's just say she was a peddler. Phyllis, let's call her Phyllis. She keeps the stock around until some guy finds himself in need of a proper sport coat - a dinner jacket even. Maybe it's for a wedding, or a funeral, or a court appearance. The point is, Jasper doesn't currently own one, so Phyllis steps in. "Well, it's a bit 'culurfool' for a funeral, wouldn't you say?" drawls old Jasper as he surveys the goods.

"Oh, not at all. It has colors, but they are all subdued by this lovely dark background. See?" Phyllis hypnotically glides the back of her age-spotted hand along the outstretched fabric.

"Subdued, huh?" asks hound dog-faced Jasper.

"Yes, solemn, but stylish!" exclaims Phyllis as she makes an exaggerated upward motion with her open hand and slender fingers.

So, our jacket's first outing was to a funeral. Poor, passed-on Haroldean stretched out in his casket. Stretched out the way Phyllis had laid out the jacket when she peddled it to Jasper. One could almost see the back of her hand passing down along poor Haroldean the way it had caressed the coat. The new jacket seeing off the old corpse.

But all this rampant daydreaming only serves to distract the curious gentleman from that most unfortunate of truths - that this very intriguing jacket was going to be at least three sizes too small. All the romantic musings on its masculine origins dashed on the rocks of petiteness. The hands will remove it from the rack and lay the fabric out the way Phyllis did, but then comes the crushing disappointment of seeing it was carved for a half-man. Life can be cruel and fashion twice as much. The let-down would be enough to make our gentleman have absurd thoughts. He'd consider befriending a pint-sized sidekick who could wear the jacket around in his stead. Our generously proportioned man would look down upon the jacket wearing jester and feel both superiority and envy. He'd

Just (the Jacket)

give the jacketeer a nickname - maybe something like "Sketchy".

"Hey, Sketchy, you get ketchup on that damn jacket and I'll knock your tuna can sized head off!" our patron of the coat would bellow. Sketchy would get all twitchy and sniff and shuffle and swear he wouldn't mess up the jacket right as he goes and wipes his nose on the sleeve! Our man of style turns livid, but then maybe he hears the laugh track and decides to shake his head in disbelief at predictable old Sketchy instead. "Sketchyyy!" he howls as he wags a finger down at him.

There's always that one in a hundred chance that it's not the case. In fact, the first inspection reveals rather wide looking shoulders. The left hand cascades down the back and is surprised how long it takes to reach the bottom. Could it be? The arms look long. Turned head-on the jacket looks like it's standing up by itself. "One feels like they should ask permission to peel back your collar and inspect your inner lining and pocket, good sir." Embroidered with class. Silk lining all intact. Perhaps a faint stain of sweat marks at the pits. Perhaps this was a clubber's jacket after all.

It had escaped death row at the normal factory. It had briefly flirted with a life of gin blossoms and bed lice but peddled its way to simple, but dignified Jasper. It hovered over poor Haroldean like it would deem to hover over all men. On some occasions, it would accompany Jasper to the bingo hall on a Saturday night. That's where it picked up its essence of cigarette. Jasper didn't know it, but the coat made him look that much more acceptable to the various widows who peppered the medium sized hall. Who knows, maybe old Jasper did ask one of them out. Maybe that jacket breathed a bit of life into the old boy. Maybe they went out and cut the rug the way neither of them had for a month of Sundays. The one-time funeral coat gave him one more shot at life.

And then came the end of Jasper. It might have

Just (the Jacket)

been the end of the coat too. Boy, it was real close. All he had left was a sister and a few cousins. None of them knew what to bury him in. Our stylish jacket almost didn't make it to adulthood after all. It was within a whisper of accompanying Jasper down into that old black earth, but at the last minute, his sister remembered that she still had one of their father's suits. She had been wanting to get rid of it anyway. That stylish, black and purple and green jacket hung on a hook and watched poor old Jasper being shoved into that dusty black suit. It was too big for him and made him look like a scarecrow, but our jacket escaped a gruesome fate.

Jasper's landlord later came in to survey the place. He'd have to get it ready for renting out again quick. Can't go too long without paying customers. He figured he should at least go pay his respects though. But what to wear?

There were only a few people there to see Jasper lowered down below, but among them was the jacket. Smart and stylish, yet somber. Simple Jasper gone, and now it was being worn on into an increasingly complicated world. It's not hard to imagine the side-dealings of the landlord. Maybe hanging out with some shady people on the wrong side of town. Always after some extra cash, the new wearer thinks the jacket gives him class. Small time dealings with big repercussions. C'mon, would it be going too far to think that maybe our jacket once took a bullet? Perhaps it was a near miss, or who knows, a closer inspection may reveal an oddly patched area. Perhaps that stain is not from sweat after all.

Seriously now, this runaway imagination thing needs to stop. One need not get so carried away just to acknowledge that this coat has been around. It is something that can be sensed by someone who knows how to feel it. No, that might be it. Those recent flights of fancy may not be far from the truth. This coat was out of commission for a while. It's the only thing that

Just (the Jacket)

explains what good shape it's in. (Please, let's not let the mind wander to some sort of "Dorian Gray" scenario where its fabric never ages!) That landlord turned petty gangster got in over his head. Maybe he took a bullet, maybe he died from the drink, but that jacket, the one he *knew* made him classy, outlived him. It was placed in suspended animation in somebody's closet. Jacket had time to think, to catch its breath. It's not hard to imagine the coat waiting patiently, like an alien parasite, to attach itself to the next host that comes along so it may resume its mission to conquer the world.

It's the 70s! Bowie and Alan Vega are on the scene. All kinds of things are happening. Bell bottoms and silk shirts with crazy designs are all the rage. Get down tonight! Arena rock. Art rock. 38-minute songs. Perms, plastic, Penthouse and proms. Somewhere in a closet, maybe even an attic closet, a jacket hangs from a rail. Generous helpings of mothballs have helped its cause. Even the bingo hall cigarettes and more from the taverns frequented by shifty landlord man begin to give way to the camphor. The house gets sold or maybe the kids take it over. The younger daughter gets it instead of the son just because she's pregnant. Her brother resents it for life.

Nest building means clean, clean, clean! And soon that attic closet gets the treatment. Unceremoniously bundled up with winter sweaters and turtlenecks, the jacket gets crammed in a garbage bag and sits there. Forever. Well, for a while at least. And once again, death swoops near. Bulging belly lady nearly just gives in and tosses the bag of clothes out with the trash. Who has time to drive it to the donation shop? Not her! But again, almost as if by the grace of God, an angel appears. A casual mention from a friend, "Oh, I'm getting ready to go donate some stuff. You have anything you want me to take away for you?", spares the jacket yet again.

And so there it sits, in a bag on the ground, around

Just (the Jacket)

back by the big receiving door. A good humored black woman named Delores puts it on the rack. She will not factor into the jacket's story again. It will hang there like a doggy in the window for some time to come. In 1977, in this part of the country, nobody wanted a jacket like that, not the rockers or the stoners or the preppies or the disco kids. Anachronistic kit. A garment caught between filaments of time. A small section of Twilight Zone on the rack where the ghosts of Jasper and others who had laid hands on it dwelt. A time traveler. A Max Ernst painting left untouched while dogs playing poker and velvet Elvis are scooped up by the armful. She's the oddly attractive girl who isn't asked out because she's too smart. A cool looking guy browses the rack, and she tries to speak to him, "Buy me and wear me to the prom. We'll stand out like some rebel loners who won't be depicted in films until the 80s. Ask a lonely girl to go with you. Pick someone no one would ever guess. Make it a memorable night for both. Sense the dripping envy in the room as they shake their heads in scorn. Your cool, vintage threads a potent antidote to their ruffles and frills. C'mon, take me. Take me out of here!"

What an embarrassing show of romanticism all because of a coat! But it's fun. It all adds a bit of spice to an otherwise mundane visit to the shops. But let's just say it was a March day and it was still plenty cool outside to make use of a jacket like this. But our late 70's rebel also had clubs in mind. Stages to stalk and birds to impress. As he parted the bland curtain-like coats crowding it, he saw enough to picture it with those thin black jeans and pointy black shoes of his. And it looked to be of good size. By the weekend our jacket had begun its new life. If such an item could achieve consciousness it may indeed have felt like it had been woken from hibernation. The social scene it knew was all taverns and smoker's coughs. Now it blew through the doors into an all black chamber of white lights and blaring music. From the down-and-

Just (the Jacket)

out to the up-and-coming the coat made the rounds. Jerky half-dancing next to a dark-haired lovely with heavy mascara. Sweat and beer. Perfumed skin pressed against the jacket.

The cool coat worked its magic. OK, maybe it was simply all around good fortune that was with our new owner that night. Heavy Mascara ended up playing a starring role. A bubble formed around them - all glamour and ease. Two young beautiful things riding the crest of a happening scene. In this non-coastal town, the normal still prevailed and these underground souls were just beginning to spread their wings, stretch their legs and shake things up. And later at home those two did shake. Fireworks. Music. Heavy breathing. The jacket, hung over a chair, looked satisfied.

While some were still going to roller rink discos and others awaited the next big arena rock show, these children from the shadows were at thinly attended basement gigs watching some weirdos with Casios and a tape machine. A new secret language being spoken. Not yet translatable to the outside world. One of the last movements born of innocence - earnest with a bit of manufactured anger, but blossoming out of a relative void. Cultural transgressions had not yet become an industry unto its own. Suddenly there was a very new kind of weird, and it was exciting. The well-proportioned, purple, black and green sport coat saw it firsthand.

It would come as no surprise if our imagined new wave punk scenester formed a band and indeed he did. He had downplayed his early high school saxophone playing once punk grabbed a hold of him and filled his head with low-slung guitars. But then he heard The Contortions and caught them at a gig in Detroit. It changed him. The band he formed was no Contortions but they held their own. For a fleeting moment in time, they did their thing on small stages in fly-over States. But it was in the rust belt that these

Just (the Jacket)

happenings felt the least tainted. No big city pressure to be super cool, just a subset of restless, creative people knowing something big was missing from life and culture and they were there to bring it. And for those suspended moments in time, the black purple jacket was there. Primitive lighting on a ramshackle stage. Four dudes bringing the air alive. Squeaky sax amid a staccato of drums and erratic guitar. Nearly a decade in mothballs, and now center stage. What would old Jasper think of that?

Esprit de corps filled the club that night. The jacket was the General inspiring the troops: "Go on, be bold, break-out, press yourselves against the screen. Let the animal roam before they cage it and sell tickets, facsimiles, knock-offs, mimics, gimmicks and scorn."

A time traveler might land there just to see it, just to feel it. She'd already seen Elvis and Janis and sat close to Simone Beauvoir in Paris, and now she shuffles on by to see this ever-so-authentic scene with lover boys and naughty girls tired of playing nice. And with time-twinkles in her eye, she turns to look at the handsome scruffy guy on stage and, ooh, that stylish jacket, so muted, so alluring, yet sated.

Oh, I know we're getting completely carried away now, but maybe, just maybe, that lucky cuss in that sport coat got extra-lucky that night with a time traveler in search of that last moment before it all went so wrong. She'd come up to him just as he dismounts the stage. And look, it's the perfect DJ come to save the day. A Blondie's tune makes it easy for her to approach and intercept. In one fluid motion the two are dancing which encourages three more and then seven. A happier, more happening little dance floor there need never be.

Time travel sex and the purple jacket. What a trip. Wouldn't be surprised if that temporally free-spirited mistress eyeballed that coat and decided to take it for a ride. Our poor up-and-coming rock star wakes to find it missing. He misses it more than he remembers

Just (the Jacket)

the girl in his bed. It did not matter who took it. It was gone. And with it apparently his mojo. Real life encroaches. Bills to pay. The dull ache of another work day.

Soon the cultural spillways filled up as it became harder and harder to differentiate style from junk. An existential crisis of the spontaneous. Predatory manufacture reigned, where each look, each movement pushes down on the heads of the others in desperate attempts to stay above water. The Age of Clicks robotized an already blanched ethos. Let's just put it this way, the time traveler, with or without the jacket, does not reappear anytime soon.

So much utterly fanciful thinking can be excused as this glowing jacket is approached by some old soul. A heady mix of nostalgia and anticipation stupefies the brain as it beholds the unknown-yet-familiar. Could it be that a garment holds the spirit and essence of the times it had? If one is sympathetic to such metaphysical ramblings, it might all play out like an old projector casting a film into dusty air. Man enters the space of projection and gets caught as if in a tractor beam. The events, emotions and beer stains of the coat's past appear as rain drops on a window next to a face. Illuminated only by street lights, the mind absorbs the droplets, simultaneously living through them all. Reprogrammed with new meaning, new memories, and a sense of chance, the hand reaches forward.

Ha! There we go again, getting all hocus pocus about a coat. But it's fun. It's good times. It helps brace for the disappointment of the jacket being small or in bad shape. Besides, is it so wrong to try to inject a little magic and wonder into this life that is otherwise obscured by vape clouds, selfie sticks and entrenched vulgarity?

The over-active imagination persists as the hand reaches out and touches the quality fabric. The way the fingertips tingle - is there some vibe in this

Just (the Jacket)

vestment? Perhaps some of our previous musings were true after all. The throbbing bass of a hundred shows. The plaintive sax. Sweat and hormones. Pheromones and energy. The fabric imbued with living memory. Every atom in every thread vibrated and agitated to an excited state that may take decades to decay. A slow wave of a Geiger counter may produce a crackle or a loopy sine wave whistle not unlike the glorious noise of experimental bands.

With surgical precision, the garment is freed. Care is taken to avoid the vulgarities to either side of it. Like taking out a "wrenched ankle" in the game "Operation", a steady hand wins the day. It slips out like a grateful baby from the vagina of an undeserving mother. A quick slap to its back and it gasps back to life.

Length: long. Sleeves: significant. Stains: not apparent. Far too many times similar gems have had ample girth only to disappoint with truncated sleeves, as if designed for some modern Neanderthal. But not this one. Its sleeves looked long enough to cover some lucky orangutan with style and freedom of movement. Yep, a guy could really swing through some trees wearing this beauty.

Like lovers dancing, the jacket is sent into a mid-air twirl. This 360 reveals no flaws. Inside, the lining is fine and shiny, and has a texture that's hard to classify, very...*organic.* One, not-quite-defect, is an odd column of indentations that runs up the spine of the inner lining. Perhaps it was stored for a long time up against something with ridges, but nothing really showed through on the back. All this would be academic if the next test failed. Left arm slides in like a warm body inside a cool sheet. Oh, yes, this is the kind of jacket that should be put on with the assistance of a striking woman. The look on her face betrays that she already knows how good you're going to look once it's completely on. Mounted as if on a stallion. Self-confident as a bull in Spring.

The left arm in. A bit snug at the bicep? Uh-oh, is

Just (the Jacket)

this going to be a narrow shoulders job? Surely, a coat like this would never have been designed for someone not already physically prepared to take the world on their shoulders. This is a decision maker's jacket. OK, if it's not exactly that, then it's the coat of a guy who knows when to slip out the back when things get out of hand. It's the style of a guy who, even though he knows your girlfriend digs him, makes himself scarce to respect your friendship. Confident that other adventures await just around the corner, he makes an early night of it.

The next big test is the spanning of the shoulders culminating in the entry of the right arm into the right sleeve. In one fluid motion, the jacket is collar-popped into place. Several rapid, exaggerated shrugs of the shoulders show that *this baby fits!* Re-adjustment of collar once again confirms who the rightful wearer of *this* coat is. The arms reach out seemingly towards nothing or perhaps to embrace the miracle of it fitting so well and escaping the clutches of the vintage boutique vultures. This was a free-range jacket that had mysteriously found its way in from the wild and onto this rack.

A sudden protectiveness appears. Not even going to take it off. Wear it to counter. Show tag. Pay. Have the girl - strike that - the cute girl at the counter cut the tag off and then wear it home. Cute counter-girl-thrift-shop-lizard. She gets first dibs on the cool vintage frocks that come in. Auntie's dress from 1969 worn with green Doc Martins. World weary at twenty-five, but smiles nonetheless. Over-sized rings. Heavy eye make-up. Those eyes. A flash of the good old days. "That's a cool jacket," she purrs as she snips the tag with scissors as black and shiny as her hair.

"Yes. Yes, it is." For a rather embarrassing few seconds the flitter flutter of teenage tummy butterflies tremble the hand reaching out for change from a ten. A muffled inner chuckle at the thought that such a pretty young thing might be interested in a dinosaur.

Just (the Jacket)

"Old enough to be your really cool Uncle," was a comeback that came to mind. Shuffle on out, old timer before you make a fool of yourself and she calls store security. "Code 5 at the checkout. Code 5!"

"Code 5" otherwise known as the "creep code". Might be a stringy-haired guy holding panties up to himself about to try them on. "Code 5! Code 5!" But it's just a geezer in a hip blazer trying to make time with a lovely who once would have been in his domain. "Twenty-odd-years younger and we'd be clubbing tonight," plays on the tip of the tongue. Shuffle on, Grandpa.

Not to worry. Once outside the sun felt great. Its rays gave the jacket a whole new life. The once muted green now sparkled like emeralds, while the purple maintained a mysterious air. This was no clown coat, more like class and style incarnate. The sheer victory of finding it deserved a ticker tape parade. Maybe that cute girl was back in there right now thinking about it. Marveling at how she had seen it purchased and worn out into the world by some mysterious guy with a future ahead (even if the lines on his face and bags under his eyes belie plenty of life already lived). A beautiful coat on a beast of a man. Ha! Who would that be kidding? Honestly, we all need to just take comfort in a bit of style and nostalgia and leave it at that. Really.

With the motions of some cool daddy-o reaching into the lower left pocket in search of a custom Zippo lighter, the hand finds a surprise. A heavy, edge-curled piece of paper. A moment spent enjoying the tactile pleasures of the little mystery finally give way to curiosity. Yellowed paper. A stub of some sort. Once withdrawn, it reveals black lettering compromised with age - "Frank's" and below that, "admit one". Aside from some black decorative scroll work at the corners, that was it. Slid safely back into the pocket, it would live to see another day.

The momentary distraction of the ticket nearly ended in a sidewalk collision. Like hippie smelling

Just (the Jacket)

salts, a cloud of patchouli formed and the face of another alluring alterna-something loomed into view. Quick apologies and moving on. But a look behind produced yet another surprise. She too looked back and gave the kind of smile not seen in many years. What sorcery is this? The power of the ego wished to minimize the agency of the jacket. Perhaps the old boy still had a spark left in him after all.

Funny how a flirtatious glance can be such a power-up. A hint of a swagger now compliments the coat and tugs the wearer slightly away from insignificance. As people age, the creeping invisibility slowly overtakes them. It's as if the cells and atoms themselves begin to weaken and slack. Little by little the background is revealed. No wonder so many believe in ghosts; they are everywhere fading to grey and often in the way. They are not spirits; they are us. Past our reproductive prime, our use is defined by the drudgeries at hand. The older we get we switch directions and become stubbornly opaque. Like slow moving obstacles in a video game, the youngsters swerve to avoid us on their way to do Very Important Things. As we endeavor to slow time and keep the Cloaked One at bay, the young pick up the pace to get to that place where they think we never ventured.

The closer people get to death the less we want to see of them. It's as if witnessing their impending fate unwittingly points us out to Death himself. He was focused on them, but now that you've presented your undeniably aging mug, he's taken new interest. A fresh protege on board. What horrors we attain when we find for a moment we've become Death's muse! The utter insult of being used by him just so he earns his title over and over again.

The elderly gather in the middle of life's ballroom as the young are a blur in the corridors, on balconies and stairs. In 18th Century French garb, the old and dying do a slow waltz as he, ever the romantic, swings from arm to arm. Gliding like a dandy through the hunched

Just (the Jacket)

over crowd, Death comes knocking and retires your dance card.

But today things are looking good. Even the puddles reflect nostalgia. Not an obnoxious modern billboard in sight, just old brick and pavement full of character and the promise of simpler times. With each step, a slight return of visibility. Superficiality brought down by increasing gravity. The expert cut of the jacket leans the torso and lengthens the limbs. The man himself becomes the focus of attention once freed from the oppression of advertisements and storefronts. The lack of cigarette or affectation shows further confidence. Just a well-jacketed man walking here. Free-handed and ready for come-what-may the wanderer belongs wherever he strays.

The gloomy, overcast sky made the whole neighborhood feel odd. Unfamiliar, though well-trodden, its heyday long behind it. Like ancient civilizations engulfed by sand or jungle, these forgotten parts of town exit the stage when the action moves on. The essence of all that happened there hangs in the air and colors the bricks. It will not cease until regeneration efforts intrude sometime in the future and vaporize the past like an atom bomb. If any morsel survives, the radiation of soulless development will sterilize it. But for now, this patch survives. Like an old person who has lost their sex appeal, it rests safely under the radar.

An alleyway to the right sloped rapidly down. Disorientating, like fractured space. With each step in that direction, gravity seems to increase a tiny bit. Everything feels ever-so-slightly more significant, including the wearer of the fabulous jacket. The bricks and pavement may look ancient but the coat feels brand new. The kind of new borne of a radical rejuvenation. It rehabilitates motion itself for the motion sick. It is the uniform of the savvy traveler. Fluid in time. No era off-limits. Pre- and post-style. Buzz-off. Get Lost. 23 skidoo. Confidence through the

Just (the Jacket)

ages. The wearer belongs to each and every town visited. Standing by this streetlight, the years flow over a sea of pavement. To be is to belong.

There we go again, getting all weird. It's just an alley from 1940s middle America. Thousands of little side roads and alleys look like that, leading off to small, isolated industrial zones that once held workshops or factories or a mom 'n pop butchers with a pony keg and a barbershop a few doors down. It was the sort of vista that was easily forgotten but one that would come flooding back in memories when stumbled upon decades later.

The wall here to the left, just tired old bricks, except for a small window with leaded glass and rusty iron bars. There are discolored areas on the wall, most of them rectangular in the shape of old playbills. The leaded glass reflects purples and browns and any attempt to see through it is fruitless. One wonders how many people worked inside the place over the years and had only that little, nearly opaque window as a connection to the outside world. Sometimes it is the rarely noticed things that best serve as portals into time. It's as if they have retained more of their past by not being looked at too much. The repeating gaze modernizes the object. If you always live in the same house, you will never experience the uncanny feeling of returning to the childhood home you haven't seen the inside of for thirty-five years. The world of appearances goes into a kind of stasis while we're not looking. If we could return to that childhood home untouched, just as we had last seen it, the vibrations of the past would be intense.

Time is short though, so one must carry on. And there at the far end of the long wall is a well-rusted sign bearing the words "Frank Street". This is the kind of moment where the hand does something before the brain even seems to command it. The left fingers slide in the left pocket and pull the stub out once again. "Frank's". Could it be? Surely, it's worth a look. In the

Just (the Jacket)

very least, one may get a glimpse of another relic from the past - a boarded up building that housed some seedy club. Perhaps it was a tavern that could have been home to the Jaspers and two-bit gangster landlords of our imagination. A peer inside through a cracked window may reveal a broken-down bar with an upturned stool where some loner would have sat drinking a beer while wearing this very jacket. Maybe the coat was pulling towards its old haunt like a lost dog trying to find its way home.

Continuing past the opaque leaded window, the old brown brick ends and Frank Street heads off to the left. Long and narrow. Looking down the road it's hard to see how far it goes. It's as if the endless brown and grey dullness of it creates a mirage. The eye can only see so far before it all becomes a blur. Most likely, it dead-ends into something like an old junkyard with rusty metal everywhere and a vine-covered truck resting on four flat tires.

Had a fog rolled in? Somehow it even smelled nostalgic. Perhaps that's what happens when things aren't painted over a thousand times. The old stuff continues to breathe. Nothing to seal in the past. No hustle and bustle to frighten off the ghosts. Speaking of ghosts, two appear straight ahead. Where did they come from? Obviously, this place isn't so deserted after all. Black fishnet stockings, torn blue jean jacket, thick eyeliner. Most important of all, the gaze of those eyes - up and down the sport coat rambler. The unmistakable appreciation - bordering on lust? Surely, this is all too much.

Once they pass, gliding through perfumed air, the head turns back hoping they look too. "This old man still has what it takes - a veritable rake!"

Watch out. Don't stumble. Eyes up ahead. Dusty, reflective glass to the right. Old shop long shuttered commands attention. Wipe away the dust. A ray of sunshine flows in. Aging man looks in and sees a setting that wakes the kid inside. Old wood display

Just (the Jacket)

case that held ties and cuff-links and little things that give men charm stands in place. The untouched past nearly intact. A witness returns to a scene. Inside he can see a woman and a boy. With their backs to him the woman picks out a coat, a jacket. A garment never wished worn. An outfit to clothe the departed.

The onlooker's jaw goes slack. This is a dangerous moment. The kind from which mojo may never come back. The pulled carpet of bad memories. The haunting intrusion of shadows past. Nostalgia spiked with thorns. Razor-sharp reminders of hardships borne. It is imperative to break this trance. Leave the young lad so both may forge on.

Moments past become the moment's truth. Push back lightly and resume. Haroldean, Jasper, two-bit gangster, dandies, and the hip tip a hat to this reflection in the mist. The baton is passed. Let not for nothing be our trials and our best. Carry on and save us from extinction once again. At this stage, any moment can become a matter of survival, especially on Frank Street.

Trusted with unfinished business, our man the vessel pulls himself away. The torso rolls. The jacket's tail a plume. A whirling dervish of concentrated experience drunk on the now. Stumbling on, enveloped in old heavy air, he makes his escape. Gravity pulls in the direction of an open door. Black hole of potentiality in sheep's clothes. Down a winding corridor he spins and misses the sign that reads "Frank's".

Each step gets heavier. Relevance. Significance. Power. Just when it seems this funhouse maze is endless, the corridor opens like an aperture and the spinning stops. All black and neon up ahead. Music. A bar. Some stools. A stage. Conversation and then people. A few here. A few over there. Two girls, one sipping a drink, look over. Now this is more like it. No skeletons. No memories. No end game in sight.

The music is nice. Might as well have a drink. Friendly bartender even compliments the jacket, then

Just (the Jacket)

the two cute girls are at either side, smiles, chit-chat. A gentle hand on the shoulder. Odd, yet witty one liners whispered in the ear. Laughs. A toast to good times. Raised glasses. A gulp of neat vodka. Light headed. Loose footed. Effortlessly gliding to the middle of the room as if on skates. Even though it hasn't happened for years, decades really, dancing comes easy. So smooth. So natural. No awkwardness. No real sense of a generation gap. The reverberating specters from the past have been defeated. The jacket and wearer have arrived. What a day!

Looks like the ice has been broken. More people crowd the dance floor. The music grows louder. What a party! Arms raised. Drinks splashed. Strobe lights. Throbbing beats. A small circle opens. People gather round. Smiling. Clapping. The center of attention. All the slick moves come effortlessly. A new girl enters the circle to dance and then another and even a swishy guy - hey, that's cool, no homophobia here - way too cool for that!

A tug on the arm. Motioning. The crowd parts. A glowing red "VIP" sign now plain above a door. The room, decked out with nice furniture, reeks of class and ambiance. Waves and shouts from a semi-circular, leather upholstered couch. Gorgeous women and a few rocker types beckon. Welcomed like an old buddy. What a place!

Drinks all round. It's difficult to hear, but it's obvious from gestures and expressions that they are all admiring the jacket. Camaraderie and champagne. Light headed. Cloud 9. This is even better than it was back in the day. It's like regaining respect after life moves on. What? The couch rotates? Surely, not enough alcohol has been consumed to make the room spin. When it stops it faces in the direction of a whole different part of the club and a band is playing! What? Really? They sound pretty good. They're playing a kind of "holding pattern" riff like they're waiting for someone to make an entrance. Sudden pressure on the back.

Just (the Jacket)

Being pushed forward. Being called to the stage! Haven't played in years, but what the hell, these are the kind of people you don't want to let down. Surely, there's a bit of the old magic left in the fingers.

Hopefully, the booze will help lubricate the old joints as well as inhibitions. As the cheering crowd parts, it feels like nothing less than a second chance to live life to the fullest, to not only exist but to be cheered...*adored.* Wow, where did all these people come from? Once up on the stage the place looks ten times as big. There was a time when having a gig on a stage like this would have been a dream come true. A roadie to the side throws a guitar from fifteen feet away - caught like a champ and slung around the shoulder in one smooth move. Must be the adrenaline. Dive right in. Play like a pro. The guitar glides along the luxurious fabric of the jacket. Sing? Yeah, why not. Catch the eye of several beautiful young things. One reaching up towards the stage. Her hand feels like silk.

Belting out lyrics straight from the heart. So full of meaning and emotion, like magic. And the riffs! Fingers traveling the neck with lightning speed. This is all that was ever needed - a break, a chance! The potential was always there, just had to set it free.

The elaborate stage lighting bounces sparkling light off the colorful jacket. The crisscross pattern of purple, green and black turns 3-dimensional, like a maze of moving, intersecting bars. Even the other musicians on stage are in awe of it and struggle to keep their attention on their instruments. They crane their heads up to keep their eyes on the jacket as the wearer is lifted up. Must be some kind of harness and wires involved. Unbelievable! Hovering twenty-five feet up in the air as the music hits a wild crescendo. The crowd goes nuts. Flushed cheeks. Eyes closed. Goose bumps.

Higher and higher. A false ceiling of lights overhead forms a giant white dreamcatcher halo. At the level of the lights the air is a glowing fog. As the body moves on, faces and forms swirl in the mist. A film of

Just (the Jacket)

countless lives plays out within the rolling puffs of dusty vapor. Jasper? Haroldean? But they descend out of sight and out of reach. Above stretches the black ceiling, spotted with the white dots of captured stars. Hovering in this dark apex the feeling of rebirth solidifies. Nagging voices crushed as triumph is savored. The roar of the crowd far below sweeps in and out like the tide.

This is that moment. It is the now that any true seeker seeks. Significance permeates every sensation and thought. In place of anonymity and decline legacy unfurls. Unbound optimism. Contentment.

Pride.

The strain of holding on to this ecstasy taxes every cell.

Ego.

May this jacket of armor hold. Let not these hot tears weaken the wings that lift the spirit and soar!

Vanity.

To reach such bliss to only see it go would be the greatest cruelty the world has ever known.

Despair.

The glow from beneath is just enough to illuminate the darkness beyond. Endless repetition. Isolated and cut off. The uncompromising abyss hangs its sign: "Enter - all are welcome here". The heavy weight of all that came before is as patient as quicksand. A final plaintive "Wait!" as gravity takes over. The apparatus begins to lower, no longer able to overcome the forces aligned against it. Arms outstretched, still clutching at glory - the star and his jacket descend from swift heavens.

But where is the stage?

Uncertainty.

The floor is round and surrounded by bleachers. At least the cheering crowd is still there.

Cheering.

Wait.

Jeering.

Just (the Jacket)

What's so funny? Even though the ground is approaching, it is obscured by two comically large shoes. And once where there were black trousers there are now garish yellow and green baggy pants. Absurd feet touch the ground. Straight ahead a fat kid points and laughs so hard he spills his popcorn. Attractive girls self-consciously cover their mouths as they too laugh hysterically. What is this, something embarrassing on the face?

A fumbling hand reaches up and unexpectedly bounces off a rubber ball where a nose should be. Spinning around in confused circles until a reflection stops the motion. A funhouse mirror of truth. There is no distortion, just the assertion that here stands a buffoon. Hair full of slide-whistles and kazoos. Cheeks smeared with monkey poo. Floppy lips that sputter "me me me" as a Santa Claus belly jiggles mercilessly. Topping off this spectacle is a ridiculously small coat. Black, purple, green and embarrassed to be seen on such a clown.

Deafening laughter. Pointing. Food flying out of gaping mouths.

Tears.

Adoration has turned her head. The next cool thing earns her attention instead.

Indifference is not invisibility, that state seems precious now. The spinning faces of judgment merge to form scorn. Ridicule and self-loathing compete; self-worth they aim to unseat. All motion stops. Profound doubt, that mightiest of adversaries stares you down.

Shrink. Shrinking. Shrunk. Receding. Desperate to disappear, to become invisible. Withdrawing down inside the jacket the head sinks like a stone below the surface of the collar. The spine pushes into the back lining like a stick being pressed down into mud. Ridicule and reduction. The cold, emotionless, self-consuming cycle of culture helps Nature sharpen her teeth. Tonight, you are the meat.

Where once there was man, now only cloth. Climbed

Just (the Jacket)

mountains at last reached with skeletal hands. Roars before battles consumed by flames. The gates of heaven a cage. Ambition flaccid. Repetition's grave. Strange victories in capitulation. What a day. Beside a pile of clothes, flesh turns to dust. With one last touch, memories imparted. From the sleeve, what's left of the self crawls out like a prince turned into a frog and quietly croaks.

Crumpled jacket on the ground. The grand circus tent goes silent. One kid sees the frog, another sees a fluttering moth. Their fathers - a nebulous quivering of air - an unwanted glimpse of the future, beware! One last indignity as the jacket belches and farts out a last breath. The comical sounds of a balloon deflating rouses one last burst of laughter and guffaws.

But with what wisdom does the toad escape?

What a day.

The thrift store crew opens the creaky back door that requires a bit of encouragement in the form of a swift kick to the lower panel. Outside on the pavement are three trash bags and two boxes stuffed with donations. In one of the boxes, beneath a pair of mustard yellow curtains, is a jacket, a sport coat. It has a stylish feel. Purple and green and black. Attractive. Different, yet subdued. Onto a cheap wire hanger it goes. Unceremoniously shoved in between cheap suits and predictable tweed. It looks like it has been around, but despite all the wounds and wrinkles, it still holds its charm.

What a day.

.

THE TARNISHED HEART

The Tarnished Heart

There were no witnesses. A mail carrier working in the suspected location recalled hearing squealing tires and seeing the blur of a white van in the distance. The abducted girl's family could not believe that such an earth-shattering event could transpire with barely a trace. [While their hearts sank like stones, the surface of the world barely registered a ripple.] The police investigated, but soon the case grew cold. An unseen abduction left them with an invisible girl. The unfathomable loss embodied in negative space followed them everywhere. She was never found. Their grief knew no end.

As dawn broke on Friday, the carnival operators emerged from their trailers and got to work on last minute preparations for the first day of business. It was a holiday weekend, and everyone was looking forward to three days of good attendance and receipts. Larry had been managing the travelling show for many years. The opportunity had come along right as he needed a fresh start. The carnival could be a pain in the ass but he was grateful that it gave him something to focus on.

Larry made a cup of coffee and stepped out of his trailer. The lush grass of the large, normally vacant lot was slippery with dew. There was a chill in the air, but it was supposed to warm up. The grass will dry. The sun will shine. People will come. They'll get thirsty and hungry and crave entertainment. Larry's operation would deliver. He liked people spending money, but he also liked to see them having fun and getting their mind off things. He knew how important that was and muttered, "Well, if I can help them out some..." he trailed off and struggled to remember the point of what he was saying and just finished his thought with an absent-minded, "Well, there's that, I suppose."

Just as he was heading off to check with Merle on the status of the bumper car ride, an old van with a large trailer pulled into the gravel lot to his right. Larry tilted his face back down towards his cup and wished he could put his whole head in like an ostrich. He turned towards the parking lot and had to use the mug to shield his eyes from the sun as it breached the horizon. Steam drifted up from the cup and made the old couple walking towards him seem like they were emerging from a mirage. The sun dodged the cup and unleashed a dazzling brilliance of light that fell like a glowing curtain in front of him. The two people then crossed between Larry and the sun and looked like black shapes from the beyond come to wreck his morning.

"Howdy," said Larry. He regretted sounding friendly because whatever they wanted he probably wasn't interested. It was too early for paying customers and too late for everything else.

"Hello there!" replied the well-groomed woman with a kind voice.

"Oh Christ, please, not more holy rollers wanting to set up a tent," Larry thought as he pondered the quickest way to get rid of them.

A gentleman in a grey suit and blue ascot came forward and offered his hand.

"Folks, I'm real busy setting up. Can I help you with something?"

"My name is Carlyle and this is Bethany. We'd like to make you a business offer."

"Look, we're pretty much full up here, and it's too soon to opening time to add anything."

Before he could finish, Bethany reached out and touched his elbow, her wrinkled but kind face illuminated by the morning sun. "We provide a very inspirational presentation. We can absolutely guarantee you that any visitors who see our attraction will exit renewed, vigorous and well, be ready to spend generous amounts of money around your fair."

"Look, I'm sure you folks have something real nice, but..."

"We'll give you twenty five percent of the receipts," interrupted Carlyle in a calm and matter of fact manner.

That quickly gave Larry pause. "Uh, how much do you charge per head?"

"Nothing," replied kindly Bethany as if it was the obvious answer. She allowed Larry his puzzled look for a moment then added, "We only take donations at the end of the attraction. People are only asked to donate what they feel is appropriate after participating in such a transformative experience."

Even though he was curious, Larry suspected that whatever this was it was going to be more hassle than windfall.

"Look, folks..."

Carlyle stepped forward and offered a fifty-dollar bill to Larry. "If you want us to leave after the first day, we'll pack up and go without a word of protest."

Larry wasn't one to turn down a fifty, but he also knew that carnival visitors wouldn't donate much of anything. They might gladly waste ten-dollars shooting at a tiny target with a rigged pellet gun in the hope of winning a one-dollar prize, but some sort of spiritual pep-talk wouldn't cut it. He also knew he couldn't trust them to be honest about how much money they took in. Carnival games don't make cash through honesty, and he expected none from them. There was some honor amongst thieves in his operation but that sure didn't mean you trust some outsider. But if they really didn't charge for their attraction he figured he wouldn't have any irate customers to deal with either. The fifty-dollar bill also had a nice feel to it.

"Just what is your attraction about anyway?"

Bethany took over. "It's hard to describe. It's very personal for us, yet at the same time is aimed to help those most in need. It's an inspirational story about a special girl who has touched many hearts."

Normally, the glimmer in her eye along with the words coming out of her mouth would have made Larry think she was coo-coo or a religious fanatic, but instead, she seemed like grandma offering him a plate of warm cookies.

He found a spot for them at the far end of the carnival. There was an unoccupied strip of grass between two noisy rides that led up to their full-size trailer. He expected them to complain about the almost invisible location, but they didn't say a word.

Things got busy and for a while, Larry forgot they were even back there. When he wandered by that corner of the lot, the only indication they were there at all was a placard that rested on the narrow alleyway of grass. It read:

"Something Heavy On Your Mind? A Transformative Experience Awaits - Enter and Exit Renewed! Donations Only!"

He stared at the words "Something heavy on your mind?" and let out a muted chuckle as the "Fury Circle" ride to his left zoomed by with hard rock blaring out the speakers. Riders shouting. Teen girls squealing. He felt dizzy. His mind was heavy alright. He'd grown to feel responsible for the people who worked the carnival. He hated the thought of letting them down - of something happening that might affect everyone's livelihood. The three armed "Whirlwind" to the right thrust a car in his direction. For a moment, it felt like it was going to keep on coming and smash through the tubular metal fencing that enclosed it. He looked and saw the face of a large, middle aged woman with a beehive hairdo staring at him from the car. She was there and then not there. Just as quickly as she came, the ride rotated her away and the back of her stacked-up hair headed off the other way. From the back, she looked like a retreating anthill.

Larry pulled himself out of his daze and thought about walking back there and seeing exactly what the old couple were up to, but the girls in the ice cream van hollered at him and he headed off in their direction instead. He then stopped by to see if Merle was still having problems with the bumper car ride. Merle was peering over the control console that worked the lights, the music and the power to the cars. He tried to be casual as he watched a pretty young thing climbing into one of the cars hoping to get a peek up her dress. Larry came up beside him and startled him.

"What?" Merle asked over the din of the ride. Once he realized what Larry was asking he shouted, "Yeah, yeah, everything's fine!" Larry knew Merle could be grouchy and had a quick temper, but what the crusty old guy really wanted was for Larry to go away so he could get back to leering in peace.

Amidst the shouts and screams and laughter of the bumper car ride, Larry looked back towards the strange old couple's mysterious attraction. Most people passed right by the sign and didn't seem to notice it, but then a woman who was with a group said something to her companions and drifted back towards it. Her friends went ahead as she stood and stared at the sign. She took a few steps forward then paused. When she was just a few feet away, she stopped and appeared ready to turn around and leave, but suddenly the trailer door swung open and Bethany stepped out. She didn't appear to say a word. She just reached a hand out towards the woman. The lady paused on the steps. She turned and looked as if to make sure she was still alone and then let the elderly woman guide her in. Larry shook his head in bemusement and walked on.

Once inside, the reluctant woman made her way into a narrow maze. Bethany took her hand from the woman's shoulder and left her. The first thing she came upon was a placard decorated with pink ribbon that read "The Story of the Little Angel Delores". There was a grainy black and white photo of a little girl in an old-fashioned dress with a distant smile on her face.

The presentation continued along the winding maze. The old couple had made good use of the long trailer. The path was very narrow like it had been made to only accommodate one visitor at a time and snaked back and forth on itself.

"This is the story of our Little Angel. We do not know much about her early childhood. We came upon her when we were travelling through America doing charity work. Little Delores was in an orphanage. The moment we set eyes upon her we knew she was something special."

A few more photos of a cherubic little girl followed. Any viewer, including the woman, couldn't help but notice a vague undercurrent of loneliness and maybe even pain in her expression. The signs went on to say:

"Once we started talking to the staff about her, it struck us that they seemed oddly put-off by the adorable child as if she was something to be wary of. These were country people and Carlyle and I chalked it up to their traditional and backward ways. We asked to meet her in person. They were hesitant, but since we had raised some much-needed funds for the institution they agreed for us to talk to her out in the courtyard. The moment we approached her, we could both sense a power about the child. Neither of us had ever experienced anything like it. She was very quiet and would only answer our questions with one or two words, if at all. When I reached out and touched her hand, a sensation shot through me. It was a feeling I had never experienced before.

Carlyle and I were silent on our ride back to our motel, but that evening we could not sleep, and spoke in hushed whispers about the child long into the night. By morning we were both in complete agreement. We must adopt her! This certitude surprised us more than anything. We had both spent so many years wrapped up in doing good work that we never even considered having children of our own. We felt that a life on the road would not be fair to them."

The woman slowly made her way along the winding aisle reading the placards. There were some large photos that showed the couple doing what appeared to be missionary work in various locales.

"At first the staff were reluctant to consider our wish to adopt the child, but we would not take no for an answer. Fortunately, those were simpler times and with persistence and a bit of paperwork, we were able to leave with the little angel. Just as we were leading little Delores out to the car, one of the ladies who ran the orphanage pulled me aside. 'There's something strange about that one, you know,' she said in hushed tones. 'The only thing that's strange is why it took us this long to find her,' was my reply. At the time, I didn't know why I said that."

The presentation went on to explain how Bethany and Carlyle soon discovered that the child did indeed have some sort of power. Over the next few years it became more evident. Eventually, anyone who got close, or touched her hand had a kind of transformative experience. Heavy hearts were lightened. Souls unburdened.

Pictures followed of happy people along with their testimonies speaking to the miraculous gifts of the Little Angel Delores. There were cheaply mocked-up photos of the child made to look as if she was indeed an angel with a halo surrounding her. Toward the end of the winding aisle, there was a solitary picture of a small casket. The woman quietly wept as she read how Delores' health had suddenly deteriorated. No doctor seemed able to diagnose her. Then, on a beautiful spring morning their Little Angel died.

"There was one country doctor we trusted and after examining her now lifeless body, he took us aside. He made us promise not to repeat what he was about to tell us. We kept that promise for many years. But now that so much time has passed we are willing to share with you what he said to us. He said that he believed our angelic child died of a broken heart. Carlyle and I were devastated. We came to the crushing realization that it now all made sense. Even though she never complained, it was obvious that our little darling somehow had the power to absorb the sadness and grief of those who touched her and that it took a toll on her. It had never EVER crossed our minds to exploit our angel, but she always seemed to bring such relief and joy to people's lives that we didn't feel at the time it was right to deny those in need the chance to receive her wonderful gifts. If we had only known that it was doing the slightest bit of harm to her, we would not have tolerated it for another second! She always seemed happy. To this day, we still carry our grief and guilt. But after much soul-searching we came to believe that if there was any way, even some small way, that we could continue to spread her blessing that we owed it to her memory."

The last placard explained how the Angel Delores had originally been found wearing a heart-shaped locket. When she got older, she always clutched it when she helped people feel better through the simple act of touching her hand. That locket was all that remained of her. So great was the child's power that some of it seemed to remain embedded in the silver heart.

The last part of the maze terminated at a velvety red curtain. The woman stepped through and stood silently in front of a display case against a wall. It was barely illuminated with a dim, tranquil blue light. The clever use of lighting and mirrors made it seem like she was looking at some sort of hologram. It was hard to gauge the depth of it - like an optical illusion. At the back of it she could just make out what looked like a pale, porcelain hand resting on a pillow. A chain, wound around its fingers, spilled forward over a satin pillow and dangled over the side. At the end of it hung a well-worn, heart shaped locket.

As she hesitantly reached into the mysterious space, a recording was triggered. A kindly woman's voice told her to reach out and touch the locket and to "unburden her soul".

The woman reached in and grasped it between her finger and thumb. The bad things she had done in life buzzing in the front of her mind like angry bees stinging at her conscience. As soon as she touched the cool metal object, she began to sob. It was like a conduit had opened between her soul and a vast empty space. As she slid her fingers over the locket, she felt a kind of electrical charge. It was as if the poison from one thousand snake bites was being sucked out of her.

Finally, she let go and stood staring at the miraculous object. Tears continued to stream down her face, and her lips quivered. No amount of confession or self-help therapy had ever had such an effect on her. Every bit of guilt and shame disappeared. She felt so different, so renewed that she barely knew herself.

She felt like she was floating when she pushed the adjoining curtain aside and stepped into the small space where Bethany stood waiting to greet her with a warm smile. Not a single word was exchanged. The woman only let out a series of hushed exclamations that sounded like "Oh, oh, oh!" Without the slightest bit of prompting, she tore open her purse and shoved every five, ten and twenty-dollar bill she had into the wooden box marked "Donations".

Larry had gotten tangled up with one of the gossipy ladies who worked the carnival, but turned his head around just in time to see the woman emerge from between the two amusement rides that obscured the trailer. He half expected her to look angry or at least bored, but far from appearing disgruntled, she looked like the happiest woman on earth.

Larry decided to see what it was all about once and for all, but just as he took a step forward Carlyle appeared to his right.

"No complaints so far I take it?" Carlyle asked him in a confident voice.

"No. No complaints," Larry responded.

"You know, if there's anything weighing heavy on *your* mind you might want to consider going inside," Carlyle said to him in a matter-of-fact way.

Larry didn't like the way the old guy seemed to be insinuating something. "Who the hell was he to imply that I have something to get off my chest?" he thought to himself. He didn't like the way Carlyle was looking at him. He felt his face turning red.

There was uncomfortable silence for a moment then Carlyle finally said, "I suppose we all have some things on our minds we would be better off without." His tone now sounded introspective.

Carlyle placed a hand on Larry's shoulder, which made him flinch. He had only half listened to the old guy because he had just spotted Merle over at the beer wagon. Merle had left his young, dim-witted nephew in charge of the bumper cars so he could get a drink. Larry hated it when he did that. Larry looked at Carlyle and mumbled something, and then the two of them set off in opposite directions.

Merle took a swig of the cheap beer and peered over the top of the plastic cup at a pair of teen girls wearing short-shorts. He figured he might as well take a bit of a stroll and get a closer look. Maybe he'd sell them a bit of weed. Maybe they'd want to go smoke a bit behind one of the attractions. He nearly caught up with them but stopped when they paused in front of the old couple's trailer.

"What the heck is that about?" he grumbled. "Good old Larry must be doing some deals on the side, eh?"

He watched the girls go in and decided to have a look for himself. Once inside, he could hear their giggling echoing back from the winding aisle. Merle paused long enough to glance at the photos and text.

"What the hell is this shit?" He looked at a picture of "Delores" with no trace of sympathy on his face. He wondered why the hell he was wasting his time when those girls were getting away. He made it to the red curtain and stopped when he heard them lingering on the other side. He pulled it aside just enough to peek in. They were barely visible in the dim blue light. They were egging each other on to reach into the weird box. Merle squinted his eyes in the hope of seeing their butts jiggle.

"This is stupid. Let's go!" and with that the girls headed for the exit.

For some reason, curiosity got the best of Merle and he bent over to read the placards once they were gone.

"Redemption. Burden lifted from your soul," he read the words out with disdain. "What's with all these damn people trying so hard to escape their past? Doesn't anyone accept responsibility anymore? You don't see me running from myself. Cowards."

He turned his attention to the glass box. He hunched down and looked in. He couldn't tell how deep it was or what was behind it. And that locket - was it worth anything? It crossed his mind to reach in and grab it. He'd show them a thing or two about redemption. Maybe he'd redeem it at the pawn shop and buy some weed with it.

"Ah, it ain't worth the hassle!" Merle waved it off and remembered that he was supposed to be hot on the tail of those chicks. He paused at the donation box long enough to retrieve the plastic covering from his almost spent pack of cigarettes and wadded it up and shoved it in the slot.

Once outside, he couldn't see the girls, but he did see Larry wandering around. He quickly headed in the opposite direction and nearly ran into Carlyle. He didn't know who he was, or he might have said something to him about the "pathetic" trailer show.

Larry no longer cared what Merle was up to. He had other things on his mind. The "ding ding ding" of pellet guns striking metal targets mimicked the rapid-fire thoughts in his head.

Merle only cared about Larry leaving him alone. He just wanted to have a beer and lose himself for a while in the noisy crowd and maybe find those girls again. The disorienting pipe organ music of the carrousel made him feel even more light-headed. "Those chicks really gotta try some of this weed!"

Carlyle was preoccupied. He gave a gentlemanly nod of his head to a plain, elderly woman who smiled at him. He returned a slight grin but only with effort. The exaggerated shrieks and cries and groans from the spooky ride to his left taunted him. He wanted to hurry away but froze there instead and let it all sink in.

The fair was bustling. Families and teenagers roamed up and down the grass. Fried donuts, french fries and cotton candy were being consumed in large quantities. A family strolled along earnestly discussing which ride should be ridden next. The daughter looked just like her. She was around eight-years old and wore a billowy white dress - just like her - just like the dress she had on the day that...

The ever-creeping guilt was like a bad drug reaction. It brought with it an almost overwhelming sense of dread that could not be vanquished. The little girl laughed. Her father put his arm around her. They were so happy - the same kind of happiness that had been denied another family forever. The guilt had been getting worse. Thoughts of suicide did nothing to relieve it. The only decent thing that remained was to contact the family or the authorities and tell them where her body could be found. At least then they could have closure. At least then they could say goodbye.

The next day the beer stand was doing a brisk business. The increase in inebriated people resulted in more stragglers finding their way down the grassy path to the mystery attraction. Whenever necessary, Bethany would intervene and encourage people to go through alone, but occasionally a couple would pass through and would almost always emerge quickly having not paused long enough to touch the locket. Usually, it would be someone alone that would venture in, often having wandered off from a group. It was as if there was a strange magnetism drawing them to the spot. It was an attraction with a specific purpose, and somehow it was those who needed it most that found their way there. Only those alone with their shame felt the need to reach into the final display. By nightfall eight people had reached in and touched the locket. Eight lives were changed. Eight souls unburdened. The donation box stuffed with bills.

The last day was busy. Families everywhere. There were also a few unsavory types. Some bikers wandered in mostly just to drink the cheap beer. One of them gravitated back to the trailer. From an observer's point of view it looked a bit silly to see the hulking man with his scraggly beard and worn leather coat pouring over the story of the delicate little Angel Delores. He should have been bored and cynical about it, but when the time came, he reached his road-worn hand into the mysterious, ethereal box and touched the heart-shaped locket dangling from the disembodied porcelain hand. The biker found himself confessing the long litany of awful things he had done. All this he blubbered in a barely audible voice as the tears streamed down his sun-ravaged cheeks. The phantom images of children left behind and victims of violence left to die circled around his head like newly liberated angels. He emptied his wallet-on-a-chain into the donation box and stumbled out. The tears wiped away to reveal a cheery, Santa Claus-like face. The other members of the gang never saw him again.

By the end of the carnival, twenty-seven people had confessed at the altar of the Angel Delores. Everything from small transgressions to crimes worthy of capital punishment had spilled forth under the spell of the simple little locket. As each confessor emerged not a one questioned the how or why of it all. The great unburdening they felt wiped away all concerns past or present. Aside from tears and smiles, the only observable reaction to the experience was the visitors emptying out their wallets into the collection box - an act they performed without pause or question. No amount of money was too great for what they had received in return.

In a town far away, a family made it through another sad day - the worst day of the year - their darling little girl's birthday.

Even though he couldn't see the family, he was always aware of their pain. He had escaped justice only to lie in bed at night in a prison of his own guilt. Freedom no longer meant anything. The combined hum of the generators dotting the fair grew louder and louder. He sat up as if catapulted, remaining attached to the bed only by a film of sticky sweat. He stumbled to the sink and gulped a glass of water.

"Enough! Tomorrow I will call the cops. Once I tell them where to find her maybe I'll kill myself. I'll worry about that when the time comes. Finally, that family will have some peace and can begin to move on." He quietly sobbed, but this time it was different; it was the sobbing of impending relief.

Carlyle walked out into the crisp night air and lit a cigarette. They had taken in a fantastic amount of money, if only he could feel happier about it. Even if he felt like he was at the end of his rope, hopefully Bethany would be all right.

As dusk fell, Larry started making his final rounds. Groups of stragglers got in a last-minute ride or bought one last bag of mini donuts. The lights of one or two attractions switched off. From a distance, it looked like a faulty bulb on a strand of Christmas lights blinking off. Larry was overcome by a wave of melancholy. It sometimes happened at the end of a run, but this time it was different. He knew it might very well be his last.

Merle threw his cigarette butt down. As he ground it into the dirt with his tattered old shoe, it seemed to sum up his whole damn life. He took a long pull on a bottle of cheap whiskey and cursed the world for not hooking him up with those two foxy chicks.

Carlyle stood and stared at the nearly full moon. It felt like time to act. Time to come clean. Time to bring this all to an end once and for all. He turned and headed for the trailer. It was time to have a serious talk with Bethany and set things right.

Larry started back towards his trailer. There was no sense putting things off any longer. But for some reason he stopped. As inconsequential as it seemed, he felt a nagging curiosity about those old people and their weird-ass attraction. The heaviness weighing on his heart was tremendous. What harm could it do now to allow himself this minor detour? The fresh night air felt good. The prospect of doing something simple like checking out an attraction that relied only on donations would help take his mind off what laid ahead. Right as he entered the narrow patch of grass leading up to their trailer, both the attractions to the left and right of him switched off their lights. Only the pale blue light that hovered like a halo above the steps leading up to the trailer door was left to guide him. For a moment, Larry just stood there staring. The remaining lights of the carnival behind him cast his shadow along the ground ahead. It looked like a black arrow pointing the way to revelation.

As Larry opened the creaky door and entered the front side, Carlyle opened the door at the back and walked in.

Larry had no idea what to expect and approached the first display with a bemused curiosity. As his eyes focused on the grainy picture of this child referred to as the "Little Angel Delores" his heart rate increased. It felt like a sick joke. Was this some sort of divine providence meant to remind him of what he had to do?

Carlyle came up behind his wife who was puttering in the small kitchenette that was walled off behind the attraction. "Bethany, I think we need to talk."

As Larry made his way along the narrow corridor, his eyes began to sting and it grew harder to read the placards. This poor child. She had led too short of a life, far too short. How could such a horrible fate be dealt out to such an innocent little girl?

"Bethany, I don't think I can go on. We have to tell the truth. We have to bring this to an end." His wife turned and looked at him with sorrowful eyes, "I know, Carlyle, I know."

Larry's hands were shaking. He was one second from turning and running back to his trailer to put an end to his torment once and for all, but something about the thick velvet curtain beckoned him. His trembling hand reached out and pushed it aside. The warm glow of the magical display case illuminated his guilt-ridden face. He reached in. It was like a fog enveloped his hand. He grasped the tiny heart-shaped locket.

Bethany and Carlyle embraced and wept on each other's shoulder. "This is it. It's gone on long enough. We'll bring it to an end, so she can finally know peace."

Larry began to mumble through tears, "I kidnapped her. I saw her. I stopped. I jumped out and grabbed her and pulled her into the van. I'm sorry, so sorry. I'll tell her family where her body is. I'll tell them so they can finally have some peace. I...I raped her. I did horrible things to her. She cried. She cried for her mommy, but I didn't stop. Then...then I strangled her. I strangled her to make her be quiet. I squeezed her throat until she was quiet. I'll tell them. I'll tell them the truth...the whole truth. This...this is the truth. I am telling it to you now, little angel, whoever you are. Little Angel Delores, I am telling you all this now. Whoever you are, please forgive me. Forgive me!" And he let go of the locket.

Larry stumbled out the adjoining curtain. Without a second thought, he pulled out his wallet and stuffed money in the box including the fifty that the elderly couple had first given him. He exited the trailer a changed man. A man free of guilt. A smile adorned his face. He would sleep like a baby that night.

Far away a family went to bed carrying with them a grief with no end.

The last of the carnival lights switched off for the night. Everyone would do their final packing up in the morning and move on but not Bethany and Carlyle.

Bethany unlocked a door and together she and Carlyle entered the small room ready to do the right thing. The back side of the mysterious box glowed a few feet away. Bethany switched on the light and the two of them sat down. They gazed at each other with silent resolve.

"Honey? Sweety? Our darling little angel. We're so sorry. So very sorry for all we've put you through!"

Bethany and Carlyle gazed down upon her. She lay there quietly - the only movement a slight quivering of her lips. The Little Angel Delores pale and sickly with untold pain displayed on her face. Countless pitiful or horrific tales projected onto the back of her eyes from every act of confession. It was impossible to tell her age. An aura of innocence blurred the ravages of corruption the way Vaseline on a camera lens softens the lines of an ageing actress. A powder blue nightgown concealed bed sores. Several empty containers of baby food sat on a small table beside her head.

Carlyle and Bethany held hands. Before he could stop her, Bethany reached down and stroked Delores' emaciated cheek. Her pleading for forgiveness changed into syrupy affection.

"Oh, look how lovely she is, Carlyle!"

"Why, yes. Yes, she is an adorable little thing, isn't she?"

The sudden change in their tone would confuse someone unfamiliar with the situation. It did not confuse Delores. She had seen it before years ago.

"How'd we do this time, mother?" Carlyle asked of his loving wife as she withdrew her hand from Delores and gazed at her husband.

"We did good. Real good. I think we'll be able to afford that new car soon. Would you like that, honey?" Bethany said to Delores as she gently removed the girl's nearly lifeless arm from the cushion that supported her hand. "Would you like that, angel? Here, let's put your locket back around your neck." A whimper escaped her emaciated mouth. Carlyle and Bethany just looked at each other and smiled.

Alone and at peace in his trailer, Larry closed his eyes ready to welcome the deepest sleep of his life. As he drifted off, he could just make out the sound of the strange old couple pulling away into the night.

The Tarnished Heart

Inter-Narrative ONE

Academic Investigator

Inter-Narrative One

Inter-narrative One

(AI5 Project Files/Library of the Damned)

This Page Intentionally Left Blank

Absolute knowledge, once breeched, comes into existence but not a moment sooner. Until then, it's merely a concept that pre-occupies intellectual gluttons, transcendental seekers, and would-be gods. Someday, one may succeed at sitting down at its table to sup, but don't be surprised if when dessert is served, it's a big plateful of uncertainty.

Inter-Narrative One

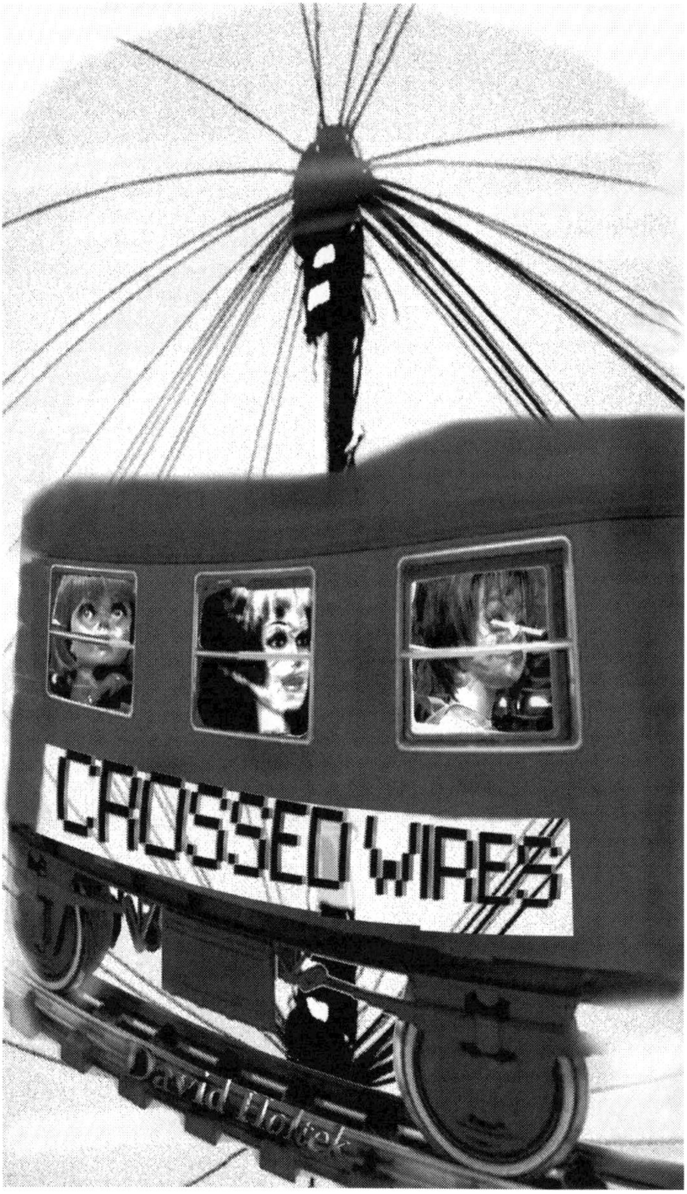
CROSSED WIRES
David Holiek

Crossed Wires

Crossed Wires

Somewhere, a guy wakes up wishing he had simply read a book in bed last night. Instead, he had stared at his tablet for an hour and ended up dreaming that his entire ceiling was a glowing screen. Even though he was asleep in a dark room, his dreaming self was sure that the glare from above was keeping him awake. When he looked in the mirror at 6am, he expected to see his face reddened by the radiation. One could argue that would be better than what he saw or at least thought he saw – a flash of words, images and emojis scrolling across the bottom of the mirror. Knuckles rubbed vigorously into eye sockets stop the hands from reflexively trying to swipe at the mirror.

A deep breath and a cup of coffee work to vanquish this technological hangover. But habits die hard as both TV and tablet are switched on. The early morning news is glanced from above and beyond the tablet as email is loaded. Sleepiness adds to the momentary confusion of words spoken on the TV appearing to be duplicated in text on the tablet screen.

It's hard to imagine why we choose to bombard ourselves with all this electronic stimuli, especially so early in the morning. It's as if our brains have begun to mutate and link up with all these glowing screens and devices that beep, chirp and notify. This isn't just like a drug addiction, it's a co-opting of gizmos and newsfeeds into our very existence. Our brains have developed an appetite for fast-food infotainment. We produce more and more devices and superficial content to jack into our skulls and project into our voracious brains, which have become acclimatized to empty calories.

Might there come a point where the devices have a mind of their own and use our increasingly dependent ones as a playground for their machinations? When will the hard drive start using us for storage? Perhaps when they need us as much as we need them, a beautiful stasis will be reached. A utopia where your phone longs for you as much as you long for it. Or perhaps it's more a hostile takeover. The AI overlords of the future have transported their tactics back in time to help hasten their ascension. Subliminal algorithms in funny cat videos. We are being seduced into servitude one click at a time.

"Must be drowsiness and crossed wires," our early riser sighs and rubs his eyes yet again. It's far too early to have convoluted thoughts like that. Fortunately, when he returns to the bathroom, the mirror has returned to being just a mirror, but for a moment the look of his jaundiced reflection makes him pine for the hallucinations.

One last possible curative for a bad night's sleep is a hot shower. No glaring screens or useless information, just invigorating streams of warm water. Even the sound is soothing. Well, it's soothing until you start to hear crackles and static in the staccato beating of the water drops. Our collective submergence into datatainment is itself like a form of slow electrocution. Our early-riser shudders and turns off the taps when the drops start to feel like ones and zeroes hitting his skin.

It just must be one of those days.

The walk to the station involves dodging the usual mass of hurried pedestrians and cyclists. As two men go about unloading boxes from the back of a truck, the scene takes on the 2-dimensional look of a pixelated video game. For a second, it looks as if one box disappears as soon as another is stacked upon it by the robotic motions of the men. "Bleep. Bleep." A noise from somewhere adds an appropriate 8-bit soundtrack to the "game play".

"Oh, dear, this must all be my brain telling me it needs more coffee," our distracted commuter mumbles to himself.

A quick detour into a coffee shop will hopefully help clear the mind. With cup in hand, a long sip brings the promise of mental clarity. It is a decent brew, but as he exits there is an odd, metallic aftertaste to it. As the door closes behind him he swears he hears the barista say, "I think the espresso machine has been hacked."

There is no time to dwell on the strange statement (if that was indeed what was said) as the crowded platform is negotiated. Station announcements mix with scattered conversations. It's hard to distinguish one from the other, but it sure sounds like someone says, "My toaster texted me!" To which another replies, "Oh, you've got one of those 'internet of things' set up, eh?" Followed by a perplexed, "Internet of what?"

The overhead speaker cuts in and out and mixes with the odd conversations. "The train arriving at platform...1011010...arriving shortly." Our commuter rapidly blinks his eyes, takes a big gulp of coffee and wonders if it's time to take a long holiday on the coast.

A small, early morning victory as a seat is secured on the train. Once settled in, a peek through the slight gap of the two seats directly ahead reveals an all too common sight. Just visible is the hand of some otherwise anonymous female holding a smart phone aloft. The other hand rises clutching a freshly loaded make-up applicator. Train as dressing room, as toilet. The terminally tardy using public space to tend to their privacies. Free of shame and committed to a singular purpose, even the shaking of the carriage does not deter them. With all the jostling and cramped space, they somehow manage to draw a black line under the eye without gouging it out - a talent wasted on vanity. Such steady, surgeon's hands could be performing brain surgery in a slightly altered reality.

Phones with their all-seeing eye have largely replaced the humble make-up compact. Instead of gazing into a mirror, we now allow the techno-cyclops to stare at us and offer up a digitized reflection. We're all stars of the small screen now. One wonders how long it will be until apps are designed that will survey and critique our looks, perhaps offering make-up advice as we go. The aesthetics of the cloud will gradually become the new benchmark. Before we know it, standards of beauty will become more machine-like. Metallic make-up tints will become ubiquitous. Contact lenses will display scrolling celebrity gossip and funny videos so more people will seek to gaze into our eyes. But instead of the opposite sex, we will strive to please and seduce our devices - if we don't, they might cut off our feeds.

Another woman, a few rows ahead, facing the rear of the train, desperately pulls at her hair trying to manifest some sort of braid. It doesn't take much to imagine the dander and dead hair cascading out into public space. Perhaps, some steward comes around to collect the discarded hairs. Once enough has been "donated", the tangled mess is passed on to some needy person. Chemotherapy or mundane baldness has created such a need, and perhaps these incessant self-groomers are merely being thoughtful and generous.

But in this world, one must be grateful that chamber pots are not made available in public venues.

In other words, nothing new on a Monday commute into work. Might as well check back in with the aspiring beauty queen. A glance through the seat backs and into the phone clutched by pearl-white, slender fingers reveals the unexpected. Instead of seeing a freakishly magnified eye or a blushed cheek freshly rouged, there is instead an outstretched arm coming up to grip the device from the opposite direction and side. It is a very disorienting sight. One might expect to see some of the girl's arm in the seat ahead leading back to her, but this was not that at all. It was as if two girls sitting opposite each other were both gripping some technological talisman with their left hands. Surely, it must be a trick of the light or a reflection from the window somehow making its way onto the girl's screen. But it is very real. It's as if they are fighting for control. But this, this digital doppelganger exists only within the small, rectangular screen.

A rapid succession of blinking to clear the eyes. A shifting of position on the seat. Fighting off a sudden onset of motion sickness. Looking around to see if anyone else is privy to this phantasmagorical occurrence. All of it to no avail as the irrational scene stays the same. It is like one hand clutching the phone has given birth to another that then extends forward into the world of the other - she herself preoccupied with the business of beautification. If someone is behind her glancing through the gap between seats, do they see the girl holding her phone in the seat ahead on this train? The mind boggles. Perhaps sleep deficiency is to blame. What a bizarre twist to an otherwise dull Monday morning!

Compelled to look away, our befuddled observer glances up at the digital scrolling sign announcing train stops. "Harlington, Brentworth....Click To See Censored Images..." "What?" As quickly as a double-take can be mustered, the words have already scrolled by. "Oh dear, surely, I'm not *that* tired", the passenger ponders with growing alarm and quickly looks away from the display. But relief is fleeting as the woman sitting beneath it is the habitual hair-puller, only now, extending down from her dark braid is what looks to be an electric cable of some sort. As she continues to obsessively tend to the braid it appears to be generating static electricity that then travels down the cable. Incredulous eyes follow it until it seems to terminate into the side of a bloke's bulky headphones. With each pulse of the cable his hand jerks up in the air and makes odd gestures with his fingers. Once one gets past the strangeness of it, there comes an intuition of it being the sign language of online shopping.

Point to select. Grasp to inspect. Squeeze to demo. Flick to discard. Stroke to add to cart.

Is it possible to stumble into some labyrinth of misreflected worlds brought on by a kind of preternatural mixing of converging realities? Has our breakneck adoption of all these consumerist technologies queered our ability to exist in the natural world? Or is this poor, put-upon gentleman suffering from an unexplained bout of hallucinations? If only there were a drinks service on the train one might be able to calm nerves with a warm cup of tea.

Our exacerbated passenger returns his attention to the anomaly just ahead of him but finds no succour. A vanity virus spreading into the virtual realm of screens and mirrors? What utter madness, yet here it is! Does she herself even know what she is looking at? Surely this is no mere hallucination. The image is quite clear. Are these creatures so obsessed with the application of foundation that they have transgressed the very building blocks of reality itself? Has eye liner mangled their line of sight? Perhaps it no longer matters to them whose face they are looking at just as long as the motions of beautification are carried out.

As tempting as it is to rise and say something to the young lady, what on earth could be said? At best, it would reveal an intrusion into her privacy. At worst, it would expose the interrogator to accusations of madness. The whole carriage would stop to see what the commotion was about. It could all be very embarrassing. Once interrupted, the phenomenon would likely disappear never to be witnessed again. Glaring eyes would silently accuse the man who dared to harass a young lady on the morning train. No. Best to just sit and marvel, to try to figure it out. Yes. There must be some reasonable explanation.

The screen jiggled. It was hard to focus in on it. The element of uncertainty was a bit of relief. This was a case where it felt preferable to doubt one's own eyes rather than accept reality. But this was not normal reality as the phone made clear once the train settled down. The disembodied woman on the screen appeared defiant as she stopped applying make-up to her own face and jerked and jabbed her tools of beautification towards the face of the girl ahead. Her frenetic motions made her seem like some sort of performance artist using the other's face as a canvas. The corporeal girl in front began doing the same. At first the flaming red lipstick in her hand just smeared violently against the screen of her phone, but then our poor commuter swoons when her hand appears to enter the phone!

As the train slowed for the approaching station, the mystery girl in the seat ahead shut off the phone and rose to her feet. So far all that had been visible was her hand clutching the phone and the other hand shuttling make-up back towards her face followed by the brief assault on her own phone. It was hard to know what to expect. Had she pulled off a miracle and done herself up nicely, even though some sort of space-altering force had taken control of her digitally generated reflection?

"Wait," our exhausted witness suddenly thinks, "is it possible she was just watching some video on her screen that made it *appear* strange stuff was happening? Have I been made a fool?"

In this case, being made a fool was preferable to being made a bed in the madhouse. But what about the other stuff?

As the train slows to a crawl, our uncertain

commuter looks out the window at a CCTV monitor showing a fish-eyed view of his train - only it is not just wide-angle distortion that greets him. The train looks like a ridiculous cartoon rendering, like a cheap video game for kids. "Surely, this is just a video too!" He tries to convince himself as he brings his hand up to his mouth in disbelief. As he does, the action on the video display reflects it. He leans closer to the window and squints. He can just make out a silly-looking face straining to look out the window of the cartoonish, undulating train on the screen. For a moment, their eyes meet.

"Preposterous!"

When the train lurches to a stop, he looks away. The girl in front is standing up. The level of anticipation nearly painful as she slowly turns to exit her seat. Hopefully she did not hear the involuntary gasp. Should something be said? Politeness compels us to say something when someone has food stuck in their teeth or when a gentleman's zipper is down. But she appeared so confident and satisfied that comment felt uncalled for. All one could do was watch her exit the carriage. Once on the platform, she turns to face the now slowly moving train as it continues on its way. Slashes of bright red lipstick look like fresh wounds across her cheeks and chin. Violent streaks of eyeliner crisscross her forehead and cut down across her eyes like black stitches. She looks like a babysitter who has fallen asleep only to be vandalized by naughty children with pens, markers and crayons.

Our present witness could not know that somewhere on a different platform, another young lady was getting off a train. Her face was also in a terrible state of aesthetic vandalism. It would have been hard to say who had won this particular battle, but one thing felt certain, this was a war that had only just begun.

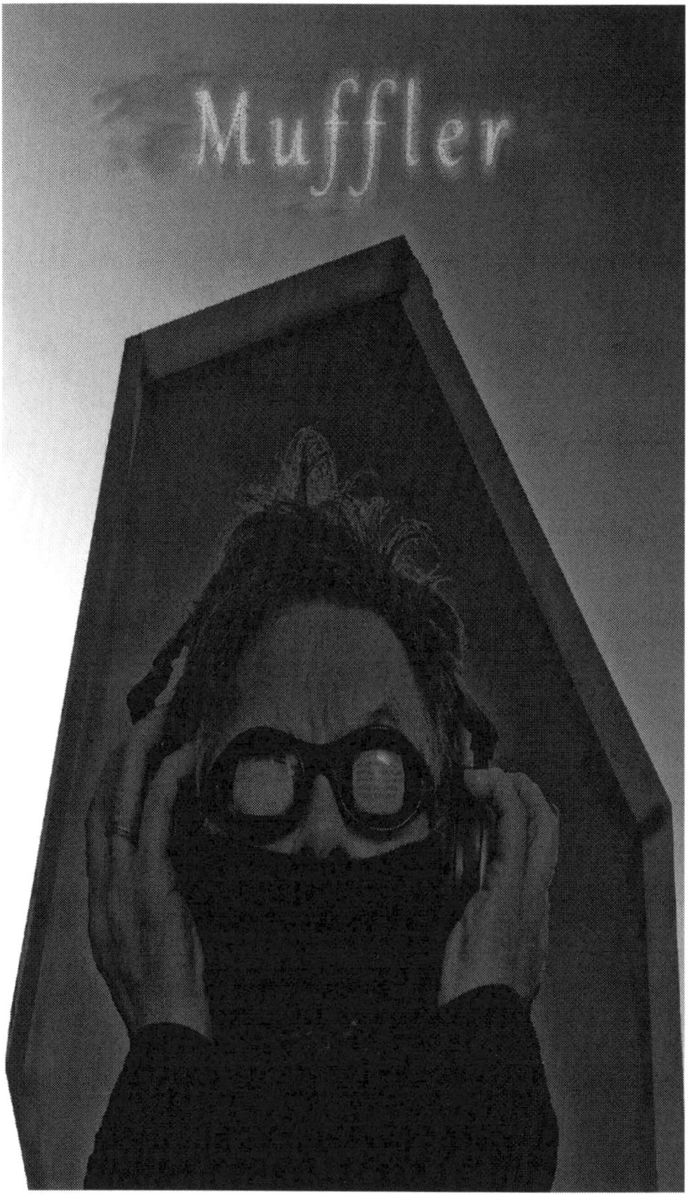
Muffler

Muffler

Muffler

"Brian, we're going to need those figures by tomorrow!" said the very Brian himself as he mimicked his boss Bobbie. What kind of a grown woman goes by the name "Bobbie"? Brian simmered to himself and again adopted a whiny, bitchy tone to mock her go-to slogan, "No excuses. No compromises!"

"C'mon, people. No excuses. No compromises!" She'd prowl the rows of work cubicles and bark like a Field Marshal in the trenches. The machine-gun-clacking of keyboards pin the cowering foot soldiers of the office down in their cubicles. The incessant screams of telephones nearly compel Brian to shout, "Medic! Medic!". As the rat-a-tat-tat of the Field Marshal's high heels on polished linoleum draw nearer, Brian believes he's hit. Hot searing pain. Afraid of seeing the damage, he has to force his gaze downward. The tell-tale darkening of his shirt confirms his worst fears; he has been hit. He sucks in air. Brian sees that he has indeed spilled piping hot coffee on himself. Trembling hands. War nerves. Shell shock.

The pale greenish lighting in the men's room always made Brian feel ill. The monotonous tile, matching stall doors and jaundiced light made the place seem like a fog of piss vapor was hanging in the air - all yellow and green, and unsterile. He stood looking at his zombified reflection. It took all his effort just to cast a reflection. His attempts to wipe away the coffee stains just made it look like he'd been sweating on his shirt in places a shirt should not be sweat upon. He gave up and wandered over to relieve himself. Just as he mounted up to the urinal, Rich from three cubes over strode in and took his own place on the firing line. It was as if he needed to announce his presence by shifting around, exhaling and making other annoying sounds. Brian froze, wishing he could disappear. He was sure Rich was going to start talking at any moment. One thing he could not tolerate was a commode conversationalist. The restroom is meant to be a neutral zone where one can see to their business in quiet dignity. Mercifully, Rich didn't speak but continued to shift and shuffle and make sniffing noises. Brian dared not ponder what exactly the insufferable slob was trying to smell.

Brian fled as soon as he could and finished the day hunkered down at his desk. "Quitting time" is a joke when one is forced to take work home. A man's castle compromised by the boss. The briefcase and laptop the new Trojan Horse. By its weight alone, the work laptop reminds Brian that his time is not yet his own. It's as if the entire office, with all its annoying details, has crammed itself into the densely packed space of the briefcase. Brian envisioned himself setting the case down on his kitchen table and opening it. All at once, the clutter of the office would fill his apartment. He'd look up to see Rich the shuffler standing in his living room. "Hey buddy, mind if I use your pisser?" Yep, the whole damn office might as well tag along.

"Fuckers!" Brian sprung a leak and cursed out loud. He had to calm his trembling hand to get his key into the door. Brian entered his apartment. Sanctuary at last. He was about to undress but stopped when he remembered he had office work to do. It was a stubborn affectation on his part to remain in his

Muffler

business clothes if he had business to do. Most would draw the line and change into comfortable pyjamas or stretchy trousers to lessen the insult of having to do work, but he was defiant. If he had to play the part, he would look the part. He would have preferred to get right on with it, but he was hungry.

Brian placed a plastic-filmed frozen dinner in the microwave. While he waited, he retrieved two stalks of broccoli and a carrot from the refrigerator. It was his way of mitigating the somewhat unhealthy instant meals. Balance was important, but one need not go overboard and be over-zealous about their diet. There is always a place for expediency and convenience.

He removed the meal and placed it on the table to his left, the fresh veg on the right. It all appeared to be in balance. He munched on the carrot while the irradiated meal cooled down a bit. The white cuff of his shirt nearly dipped into the steaming meal, but he jerked it away just in time. Careful. Haste makes waste.

The white table. The sickly white fluorescent light. The stained white shirt. His pale face. Brian had succeeded in mimicking the workplace. He looked just as he does in the lunchroom - a lifeless automaton consuming just enough food products to maintain a functioning metabolism. At work he always eats early to avoid the onslaught of the other employees. Their stinky food and spastic mastication drives him to wit's end. They sit there and talk about useless garbage with their mouths full. The bits of food flying about the only thing of any substance coming out of their maws.

"Did you hear about so-and-so doing such-and-such?"

"Did you watch that inane television show last night? You know, the one about stupid people doing stupid things?"

Or food. Brian loves it when they sit there rhapsodically talking about food *while they eat food.*

"I know, let's compare lunches!"

It's like they're sharing and showing off pictures of their unpleasant children except it's leftovers in Tupperware.

"Ooh, I've simply GOT to have that recipe," as the flakes of food and spittle cascade out of their collective mouths. Brian figured they'd gush over rat poison if only you garnished it with parsley and a radish floweret.

Brian realized how hard his jaws were clenched when the pain snapped him out of his work-hate-trance. He still had some eating to do himself before he got to work, and his wandering mind was not helping. He ate the raw veggies first. Surely, even feigning balance had some value in this world. One must keep a clear head when bad choices abound.

Continuing with the theme of replicating work settings, Brian took his briefcase over to the old wooden desk in the corner of the living room. Out came some papers along with his work laptop. Soon a hastily prepared cup of coffee would join the ensemble. Brian had allowed himself a calendar on the wall of his "home office", but he was damned if he'd go as far as putting up pictures of a fake family. There was no denying that it would make it more authentic. He didn't have any at his actual place of work either but everyone else did. The place was like the waiting room of a cut-rate family photographer's studio. Felt cubicle divider walls pin pricked with push pinned pictures of people locked in a state of denial. Little bits of their souls trapped at work with some "loved one" who must not love them *that much* or they wouldn't have subjected them to the shared purgatory of servitude even if only in picture form. Smiling children just seconds from erupting in terror at the specter of their own future - strapped to a computer workstation with their own photographs of their own cursed progeny. The endless cycle of imprisonment sweetened with the promise of a phantom home life. Cutesy pictures of pets who would never put up with what their owners put up with at work. Fluffy does not care that your eyes hurt from the strain of staring at a monitor, but if your carpal tunnel prevents you from endlessly petting them, they will take notice. Everyone is just fine with you being there and not at home, but go ahead and pin up your little photographs and pretend like you're looking out a window at your real, authentic and fulfilling life. Bring-your-false-hopes-to-work-day.

Brian knew if he concentrated he could get the extra work done in a couple hours and still have some semblance of an evening to enjoy. He zeroed in on the spreadsheets and unprocessed data and got to work.

"Let's see, if I insert this formula into cell..."

"THUMP THUMP THUMP!" A sound from the ceiling broke his concentration. He had seen signs of someone moving in last week but hadn't given it much thought. It hadn't been easy finding an affordable place in this area, and one reason he jumped on it was the high ceilings. Normally, even if upstairs neighbors were a bit loud the high ceilings would act as a barrier.

"Well, hopefully THAT was a fluke," he reassured himself and got back to filling cells.

"Bumpa-thumpa-thump." The unmistakeable sound of clumsy feet running across a floor. Brian's blood ran cold. "No, not that. Anything but that!"

Beads of sweat. Fingernails curled under and made rude contact with the wooden desk. Holding on for dear life that this moment too shall pass.

"No. Please, no." A flash of horror rocked Brian in his chair. He was robbed of the momentary comfort of denial when the ceiling vibrated yet again from the force of a herd of one forging its barbaric path. A scorched earth policy was being enacted right above his head. What should have taken maybe an hour and a half to complete took Brian over three hours instead.

The coming days found Brian pale of color and anemic in gesture. The continued trampling from above came to him like a cancer diagnosis. Could life really be over? Was this it? The sanctuary of the home violated. Invaded. Disrespected. Burnt to the ground.

"Crunch time, people! It'sss crunch time!" The Field Marshal drew out the "s" the way a ring announcer would introduce a big bout. Brian had also heard her refer to it as "show-time" in the past. She was a master at making the already unpleasant twice as unsavory. This was the big client. The most important project of the year. It would be weeks before it would most likely get wrapped up.

"No excuses. No compromises!"

Blazer and skirt. Skirt and Blazer. Dark grey with speckles. Navy blue. Black. Chartreuse for the days where the office spends five minutes celebrating an employee's birthday. On most occasions, the Marshal will give the lucky birthday bunny the newest top selling self-help book on the market:

1000 Tips for Success in a Culture Blindly Obsessed with Success.

How to Reach for the Stars Without Inadvertently Plunging to Your Death Instead.

Great Advice on Ways to Ask for a Raise So That You Don't Feel Humiliated When You're Inevitably Turned Down.

How to Project the Unmistakable Body Language of the Successful and Predatory.

Take No Prisoners: How to Tell Potential Allies from Enemies-in-Waiting (and Tips for Enlisting Soldiers in Your Battle to Succeed).

Ambitionitus - How to Not Catch the Disease of Mediocrity from Lazy Co-workers.

And if the birthday boy or girl was real lucky they might get called into the big office for a personalized, inspiring message. If her words didn't get through to you, maybe the ever-changing motivational posters on her wall would.

Success is the Greatest Holiday.

Complaining is a Symptom of Failure.

The Front of the Line is a State of Mind.
Reward Yourself by Working Harder.
And then there's the ones bordering on nonsensical philoso-babble:
Turn No into Nothing.
If You Have It in You Why Aren't You Using It?
To the downright obscene:
Act Like Your Ambition.
The Distracted Get Trampled by the Focused.
Respect - Just Like Your Pay Check - Must Be Earned.
Any time Brian had to go into her office it would take the rest of the day to shake off the feeling that he'd been lobotomized. Often, he'd ponder designing his own mottos:
Motivational Posters Make Good Kindlin.
Real Problems Can Always Be Solved by Trite Platitudes.
Failure Has Feelings Too.
Success is Measured by Body Count.
Collateral Damage is Evidence of Achievement.
Brian had many more, but the austere calendar on his fabric-covered cubicle wall was all he'd allow himself. It was a kind of silent protest. This was not his home and he was not going to try to "gussy it up" to make it pass for anything other than a work place. If anything, he could do with some sort of de-motivational posters:
Murdering Co-workers Results in Massive Red Tape - DON'T DO IT!
Giving Up is Its Own Kind of Success.
Aim Lower Sleep More.
Despite his disdain towards all the vacuous, corporate sloganeering, Brian was determined to get as much done at work as possible. He figured he could rescue most of his evening if he could only finish up this current batch of data.
"Crinkle, crinkle. Riiip. Rustle, rustle. Crunch, crunch, crunch."

Muffler

The woman sitting behind Brian started in on a bag of potato chips. With every noisy bite, he had to regain his concentration. After every third chip was violated in her mouth she followed up with a "slurp" of her fingers and a smack of her lips. God forbid that even a tiny streak of grease and salt might escape her gob. Finally, after what seemed like hours, the molested bag was crinkled up and thrown in the trash.

Brian managed fifteen seconds of concentration before she made wet chirping noises in an apparent effort to dislodge and consume wayward crumbs that had momentarily found refuge between her cheek and gums. Take no prisoners. Ferret out each and every morsel and send them on a death march towards the gut. He didn't have to turn around to know that she was now using her stubby fingers to root around in her mouth like a plumber using a metal snake to clear a septic tank drain. His concentration was shot.

Home. Microwave. Two servings of fresh vegetable. Unusual craving for beets. Roll chair up to desk. Work.

"Thump, thump thump thump." On and on it went. Even if he managed to ignore the sounds, the vibrations undulating through the desk would be his undoing. The space above his apartment had been vacant when he moved in. The landlady had informed him that she mostly used it for storage. Now, something far more evil had taken over the space. Again, what should have been wrapped up by 7pm took him until 9:30.

The next day on his lunch break, Brian decided to make a quick dash to the hardware store. Just as he was about to turn the corner and duck down the stairwell, the Field Marshal came out of the elevator.

"Oh, where you running off to, Brian?"

"Just need to do a quick errand."

"Oh. (pregnant pause) You know, I've found that it often takes extra time for people to get back into the swing of things when they leave the building for lunch."

"Yeah, I find that it often takes me extra time to get into my home life after I've spent three hours doing office work at home."

"Brian." She looked at him over the top of her fashionable glasses with the faux purple mother of pearl plastic at the sides. She had a few different pairs designed to match the temper of her business suits. These proved that she was fashion-forward, a serious business woman with a serious sense of style. She observes your level of distraction when you come back from lunch OUTSIDE THE BUILDING with the aid of smart, contemporary eyewear. "Brian, you know it's crunch time around here and a positive attitude is key to getting the job done."

Brian shuddered to think that inevitably she would turn everything into an acronym and catch-phrase.

"People, let's cut down on LOBs! You know, 'Lunches Outside the Building'. We have a perfectly good break room right here with a refrigerator and microwave. If you don't have time to prepare your lunch in the morning, maybe you're not managing your time well. When we're all present during lunch breaks there's a greater chance for synergy and team building."

Brian made a break for the stairwell. The Marshal was already barking some other prop-a-company-ganda at some other poor soul. When the fire door slammed shut behind him it was like her shrill voice had become trapped in the stairwell. Brian hurried and almost fell.

"Brian. Brian! No LOB'ing! Brian, I'm coming down the stairs after you, Brian, to make sure you are instantly in work-mode when you return!"

The yellowed fluorescent lights and grimy tile gave the stairwell a morgue-like atmosphere. The sound of her was still behind him. He twisted his head to see snake-like undulations of grey tweed darting back and forth like eels swimming downstream. And there hovering in the thick of it was a pair of emerald green-rimmed designer glasses with featherweight lenses. Glowing, menacing eyes peered through them and stung at the nape of his neck.

"Brian, there's currently no meetings being held in the stairwell. Why are you here? I hope you're running down the stairs to invigorate yourself for a long afternoon of work. The clients always take the elevator. It's a good place to put them at ease by making a joke about the weather. Look into my glasses, Brian and I will show you the magical beauty of completing projects on time and under-budget."

Brian burst through the door that lead into the lobby and reception area. The sunlight that poured into the stairwell mercifully banished the specter of the harpy chasing him down the stairs.

The startled receptionist at the front desk looked like she expected him to be holding an assault rifle or screaming "fire!". He might have been tempted to shout "harpy!" but gathered himself and coolly strolled out of the building.

Of course, there was traffic. At a light, Brian got stuck next to a car cranking rap music out the window. He managed to edge up some and ended up beside a girl listening to the latest assembly-line-produced pop music at equally offensive levels. A glance at her revealed a head that had swayed, and was now swaying to the same melody and song structure of everything else she had ever listened to. Oh, and of course, she was singing along. The already vacuous lyrics made blander by the anemic accompaniment of her failed, yet earnest attempt.

The cruelty of life exists in the nefarious reverse osmosis of shallow into deep. They're the fundamentalist at your door. The offensive odors of a shopping mall food court. It's the sound of a baby crying out of the left speaker of your Coltrane. It's the beast of lowest common denominator breathing down your neck and spitting in your ear. It's the seepage of bad into good. The muddy footprints of the braggarts,

Muffler

laggards and just plain lousy. Their symphony is a car alarm. Their calling card a bee sting. Always a sweaty handshake before they shake you down. Culture confiscation units. Robots running on shitty code. Rats in the sewer system of life. Swamp gas in your oxygen line. If you're too far away to smell their farts they will beep at you. They will cross the mall to envelope you in the World War One trench warfare chemical fog of their fifty-dollar perfume. If you try to go live in a cave, they will seek you out, hunt you down and bag their quarry - a selfie with the "freak in a cave" so they can "post it" on their online world. Another successful kill. Another anomaly dragged into the sterilizing light of day. The day of the deadly bores flooding under your door. The brown water from the bottomless wellspring of the dull. It wears you down. It pisses on your senses and shits in your soul.

Brian roused himself from his internal rant, and the blood gradually returned to his now unclenched knuckles as his grip on the steering wheel relaxed. He pulled into the parking lot and entered the hardware store.

"Aisle five," said the clerk in an odd, sing-songy voice without even looking up at Brian.

There next to the work gloves was a smattering of ear protection from spongy buds to bulky headphones. Brian sure didn't want to have to wear those around, so he grabbed a pack of the orange ear inserts.

"Is that it for ya'?" asked the terminally casual young clerk.

"Yes."

"These things are good for concerts, ya' know. I stood right next to a wall of speakers on Saturday. If I hadn't had these in I think my ears would have bled, man."

"Oh, is that so?"

"Yeah, man. I mean my clothes were vibrating it was sooo loud," and with that he made "buh-da-da-da" sounds and thrust "devil horn" fingers up into the air.

Muffler

Brian's nostrils flared with disdain. His mouth contorted to reveal gritted teeth as he peered down his long, angular nose at the clerk. Brian suspected that the youth had emerged out of that "wall of speakers" like a birthed worm. The noise alone was not offensive enough; it gave birth to this simpleton. The excretion of low-brow culture. An army of body-snatched blithering idiots giving arms and legs to rude sounds. Pull back the curtain and you'd see a hideous blob belching his kind out like mucous covered eggs. It is the mother of all things base and annoying. The beast that ensures the bloodline of bad taste. A monstrosity farting methane as it pushes its filth out into the world. It is immobilised by the mass of its own indecency so it vomits up the likes of the clerk to chase you down and thrust devil horns in your face.

Brian's only response to him was, "I wish I already had them in."

He tried to slink back into the office, but there was the Field Marshal making a show of looking at her watch and raising an eyebrow when she spotted him. It had taken longer than he expected, so he quaffed down a few bites of lunch at his desk. It would be take-your-work-home-night yet again.

A serving of fresh vegetables followed by microwave meal. Move to the big desk and knock-out an hour and a half of work. Concentrate. "THUMP THUMP THUMP THUMP THUMP!"

Brian's fingers formed a death grip on the mouse. His teeth mashed together like an angry vice. The earplugs. Thank god for the earplugs. He fumbled in his pocket for them. Not there. He rifled through his briefcase. Not there.

"Damn it!" Brian strained to peer into the recent past and saw himself toss the small plastic package onto his desk at work where they undoubtedly still were at that very moment. "All that for nothing!" He tried to keep working, but the stomping compromised his every thought. When the whole ceiling rattled he slammed his fist on the desk and pushed himself away from it. In the medicine cabinet he found a pill bottle containing a wad of cotton. He tore at it like a starving animal would a piece of meat and shoved as much in his ears as he could.

Even though it muffled the sound, he could still feel the vibrations of the stomping. Veins throbbed in his head as he mustered every bit of determination he had, but as soon as he'd start to make some headway the ceiling, walls and floor would rumble from the weight of the Thing Upstairs. His spreadsheets appeared incomprehensible. The tables of unprocessed data a swarm of ants carrying numbers on their backs.

When Brian arrived home Friday evening, the landlady was standing in the parking lot behind the building. Brian approached her. "Excuse me."

"Yes?" she responded by closing her eyes. She was one of those people who lower their eyelids like blackout curtains for inordinate lengths of time when you're trying to tell them something they probably don't want to hear.

"Obviously, someone has moved in above me and well, they're pretty noisy. Lots of stomping around. It's hard for me to concentrate. Is there..." but before he could finish the eyelid lady cut him off.

"Yes. That happens to be my daughter and my precious grandson."

What's with the closed eyes? Is she so enamoured with her "precious grandson" that she has a portrait of him tattooed on the inside of her eyelids?

"I just wish there wasn't so much stomping."

"Look. He's a child. There's no rules against children in the building."

Brian was growing ever more frustrated and speaking to a woman who looked like she was defiantly feigning sleep with her purposefully sealed eyes only made it worse, and he blurted out, "If that's the case I may have to look for a new place."

Muffler

"I'm sure I don't have to remind you that you recently signed a one-year lease and that you are legally bound to it." A tremolo shaking of her head accompanied the sealed eyes this time.

Brian wondered if she could in fact see through the lids and the whole thing was a ruse. He scratched his chin and the next time she slammed them shut he extended his middle finger while he pretended to scratch. No noticeable reaction on her part.

He ground his increasingly worn teeth. He knew she was right about the lease, and he knew damn well he couldn't afford anything else in the area. He was lucky to have found the place. At least he used to be.

Old eyeless decided she needed to rub it in a bit and advised him to work his schedule around precious' play time. He wondered if she ever films herself to see what she looks like to the rest of the world. Does she do that when she drives? Is the world too bright for her? Does she believe that things will disappear if she can't see them?

Brian remembered to bring the earplugs home this time. The banging from above was ongoing when he entered his apartment. He reached into his pocket and pulled the plugs out. His hands were trembling as he tore into the plastic like a junkie fumbling with a fix. He ate his portion of fresh veg and microwave meal in muffled silence. But once at the massive wooden desk, the stomping and thumping from above still penetrated his personal space. He tried shoving the earplugs in further to no avail. With each bump, the vibrations also registered through the floor and shot up through the legs of the desk and disturbed his arms as he attempted to enter crucial data into tiny fields.

Brian's anticipation of the next reverberations from above became as bad as the noise itself. It was like watching a nurse slowly approaching your extended arm with a needle to extract blood. Anticipating what was coming made it nearly impossible to maintain concentration. Sometimes the loudest thumps were quickly followed by the muffled sounds of a kid crying. Boo-hoo-hoo, baby fall down. Brian found himself wishing for a moment of abject silence after such a tumble that would then be followed by a mother's shrieks. He'd put up with the racket of a screeching ambulance if it meant hauling the...*thing* away. But it was invincible like a club-footed gollum made of clay. Sometimes the strikes against his ceiling were so loud that he expected the thing to break through and come crashing down onto his floor. He felt that if such an event did occur, he'd have the right to treat it as an intruder and bludgeon it. "It all happened so fast, officer. I didn't have time to make out that it was a small child. What with all the news in the world I assumed it was a terrorist."

The next day at work, the Field Marshal appeared at his desk. He heard her coming, of course. There was no ignoring the "clack clack clack" of her power heels on the hard linoleum. As the din approached he half expected her to be mounted on a snorting black stallion that would rear up as she stopped beside his cubicle. Napoleanna dismounted and invaded his space.

"Uhm, Brian."

"Oh boy, here we go," he grimaced to himself.

"Jason is off sick with a cold and Terry got called away on a family emergency, so I'm afraid there's some slack you'll have to take up on the project."

A lump formed in Brian's throat and a bead of sweat appeared on his forehead. "Look, I'm doing two to three hours of work at night on my own time as it is."

"Brian, there is no 'my time' when it comes to projects as important as this one. If everyone had that attitude we'd lose accounts and go out of business. I guess then you'd have plenty of 'my time' if that's what you're after," said Bobbie as if she were lecturing a selfish child.

"I'll have Janice send you the data."

Muffler

Brian gritted his teeth for what he *knew* was coming next.

"Remember, Brian, no excuses, no compromises!"

As the sound of her heels clattered off into the distance, Brian stared at his inbox. Within a minute they began to appear like cyber death threats in some teenage internet horror movie. One, then two, then three. They materialized into existence on his screen like severed heads bobbing out of a murky lake.

"Data set 1. Data set 2..."

The innocent sounding subject lines effectively destroyed his weekend.

Brian did his best to stay calm. During the drive home he resolved to get right to it. He figured if he could crank out four hours of concentrated work he could then salvage something of a weekend. He'd still have to do more, but the pressure would be off. He felt OK. He even decided to rush right into his apartment and put his laptop down on the big desk and fire it up. He'd put dinner off and instead make a cup of coffee and do an hour of power work.

The reassuring darkness of the coffee calmed him. He hovered over it to savour the fragrance and the heat. It conveyed the tranquillity of a lake at midnight, its surface still and inviting. Then Brian's kitchen became the scene of a dinosaur blockbuster movie. The trope was horribly clichéd and he grimaced at its vulgarity. The first hint of impending doom a ripple in a cup. The transcendental serenity of the cup jarred back not only into reality, but hell. Like turbulence on a plane, anticipation of the next jolt was worse than the turbulence itself. False hope lasts but a moment until the surface ripples again. The beast is upon us.

The chaotic steps of the thing upstairs turned the surface of the coffee into a series of endless ripples. Brian grabbed the cup from the table to make it stop but only succeeded in splashing the hot liquid onto his hand. The scalding sensation was met and amplified by the shock of a rumbling floor. It was as if the club-footed stomping of the thing exactly matched the structural resonance of the entire building. His surroundings were a tuning fork and the beast was striking it over and over again in a fit of sick glee.

Even with the earplugs pushed dangerously deep into his ear canals, Brian could still hear the muffled stomping as well as feel it. A Friday evening doing something he didn't want to do in an environment he now found excruciating.

The fingernails of Brian's left hand became intimate with the soft, aged wood of the old desk. The cheap plastic mouse creaked as he tightened his grip. "Thump, thump". The world continued to quiver from the erratic plodding thing from above. He couldn't even just get up and leave. He was a prisoner to the work and a victim of the Chinese water torture of the unpredictable stomping. As soon as he'd manage to execute a moment's work, his concentration would be rattled. His planned few hours of work turned into the entire evening. Even when the stomping ceased, the silence was soon violated by the muffled sounds of crying. By the time that finally ended, it was well past 9pm. He had been up since 5am. Even with relative peace, it was hard to think. He gave up at 11:15 and went to bed. Brian laid there and stared into the darkness. He could feel each beat of his heart. He closed his eyes. Each thump in his chest synced up with the sound of the thing's stomping that was trapped in his head like an undead echo. It was too late to prevent the inevitable slide from reality into nightmare.

Brian was addressing a room full of people sitting around a large table. All eyes were on him as he struggled to makes sounds. Each utterance was incoherent. He stuttered in time with sharp, repetitive blows to his leg. Dream-state Brian pushes back from the table and looks down. Peering up from the partial darkness is an impish little kid kicking Brian in the shin. "Smack, smack, smack."

Muffler

"Smack, smack, smack." Brian's left eye opened. The noise from above served as his horrifying alarm clock. There was no snooze button to fend off the dread. From nightmare to reality and back again. There was no sense trying to get more sleep. It wasn't just the stomping, the specter of all the office work he still had to do haunted him.

After breakfast and coffee, he tried to get some work done, but the irregular noises and vibrations made everything take three or four times as long. His jaw was beginning to hurt from being constantly clenched. He slammed the laptop closed so hard he feared he might have broken it. He had to get some fresh air. He remembered the large headphones from the hardware store. Maybe they would do the trick. He got in his car and drove.

"Oh, hey, man!" the overly talkative heavy metal aficionado at the counter recognized Brian and gave him a wave. Brian barely looked at him and made his way to the relevant aisle. The bulky headphone-style ear protectors caught his eye. Maybe these were the cure for his misery. He held them. He rotated them around in his hands. He caressed them.

"Oh, wow, bro, you must be doing some loud work. First the plugs and now the headphones. You blowin' up your house, man?" The kid was just "being a dude" but Brian found his over-familiarity insulting.

"No. As a matter of fact I'm trying to block out loud people. Rude, loud people." Brian's withering look made him appear even more beat and weathered. His sarcasm was lost on the teenager who was mostly feeling sorry for him all of a sudden.

"Oh, man, that's a drag!" and then his face lit back up. "What you should do, bro, is crank some death metal whenever they get out of hand. Let 'em deal with THAT!" And he made a vaguely hip hop-ish gesture with his hand that belied a bit of cultural confusion on his part. Brian peered down his nose at him and saw a kind of Frankensteinian abomination. A thing of youth

Muffler

that only functions via media-acquired affectations and never learns basic concepts like respect or personal hygiene. If it wasn't fed input from glowing screens it would stand in a corner and drool on itself.

There was an odd pause between them after the clerk handed Brian the headphones in a plastic bag. Brian stared at him with dead eyes and eventually said, "maybe I'll tie them up and force them to listen to silence for a few days."

"Uh, yeah, dude, that's cool." And they parted company.

Brian wasn't home for five minutes before he was forced to don the headphones. At first, he was hopeful, but even the bulky, twenty-five-dollar pair couldn't stop the vibrations from rattling his bones. He did his best to carry on, but each "thump" from above destroyed his concentration. After one excessively loud bang, Brian tore off the headphones, slammed them down and headed for the door.

He tried his best to regain his composure as he went out to the landing and headed up the musty smelling stairs. Brian took a deep breath before knocking on the neighbor's door. He knew he had to be careful not to bring on the wrath of the landlady, but he was at wit's end.

As he knocked on the door, he could hear "the thing" bouncing around just inside. A woman opened the door. He had half spotted her a couple times before, but this was his first close-up. She not only looked like her mother but when she opened the door she only briefly glanced at him before she closed her eyes and said, "Yes?".

Great, another eye-shutter. "Look, I live downstairs, and all the stomping is making it a bit hard to concentrate. Is there any way that…"

"Excuse me, I have a young child in here, and I'm most certainly NOT going to stop him from playing or walking around my own apartment." Her eyes were

Muffler

either shut or fluttering in and out of a half-open state throughout most of her sentence.

"Look," Brian said in a tone that revealed the raw desperation of someone about to try to reason with someone wholly unreasonable, "all I'm asking for is a little consideration."

"You know," Close-eyed Sally cut him off, "my mother told me you might be a problem and," - here the eyes shut in a way that communicated utter disdain for him, like she already had the complete measure of him and was just barely mustering a reply – "she was totally right. You're a complainer and a troublemaker."

As Brian tried to manage a word, the eyelids fluttered with a speed that would have attracted hummingbirds in heat. Her spider leg-like eyelashes twitched as if in seizure. It all appeared utterly grotesque to him. It was like a sea of previously invisible mites and other parasites had gained critical mass and turned her lashes into a sea of motion, like shag carpet teeming with maggots.

"Nuh-uh-uh," she protested, "this conversation is over and if you bother me again I'll have my mother evict you."

Once back in the confines of his apartment, it seemed obvious that the blinking shrew upstairs was encouraging her spawn to run and stomp as much as possible. Brian pictured her dangling sweets aloft tied to the end of a stick, with the corpulent abomination stumbling from the dizziness of turning tight corners to chase the treats. Mommy's infested eyelids quivering as if in REM state play out images of Brian under torture in the flat below. She takes the grin of a mischievous schoolgirl tormenting a baby brother. She lowers the stick to let Baby Frankenstein finally catch the carrot, only it's not a carrot because he hates veggies. It's a bon-bon.

Brian's left shoulder rose well above his right to reveal a contorted man. Even with the noise reducing

Muffler

headphones on he could hear the child gasping for air as its teeth grasped for sugar bits, or rather, Brian imagined he could. Unable to stand still, the Thing Upstairs stomp-marches in place like a dreaming dog treading the couch, covering no ground, yet compelled to make the motions by a brainstem free of any cortex control.

On Monday morning, baby lead-foot beats Brian's alarm clock to the punch and rouses him from deep slumber. He exits his apartment to the sounds of the stomps. On the drive to work, a jackhammer continues the groove. In the lobby, a guy in coveralls bangs a nail into a wall. He keeps time even as he looks over his shoulder at Brian. Then the bastard goes and does it. Manly guy with a half-beard and boxer's nose flutters his eyelids. Brian looks down and swears he can see the guy stomping his feet in place.

Brian gives one more look back to see what he's hanging. An expensive frame that probably cost more than his week's salary enclosing the simple, yet profound words, *"No Excuses. No Compromises."*

On the hard stairs going up, Brian tried to alter the fall of his own steps so they weren't in time with the hammering. He didn't have to go back and look to know that the worker was now just hammering the side of his toolbox for effect. It was like the fuck could see through the stairwell wall and was able to match the rhythm of Brian's steps. Brian became so aware of it that when the guy did a quick, erratic beat it caused Brian to nearly tumble down the stairs.

Damp with sweat, Brian burst through the door into his workplace lobby. The din of the hammer followed him, but a new element took up the rhythm. The sound of the Field Marshal's heels click-clacking the tile delivered the crescendo. The fact that she did not break form and seamlessly came at him clutching print-outs proved that she too could see through walls and knew he was coming. They were all tied in like a psychic cabal. The monstrosity upstairs had handed the baton off to the worker, and now he to Bobbie. He was positive that at that moment his apartment was blissfully quiet and would remain so until he returned.

The additional work that she had handed him would have been ridiculous if not so tragic. Brian's fingers felt cold and lifeless when he took the papers from her. It was as if a lieutenant having already been put in charge of a suicide mission was handed, at the last minute, a supplementary order to water the plants before he set off.

"Your orders are to penetrate the enemy line and advance to the heart of their operations. Once there kill all the generals. Oh, and make sure you change the oil in the jeep before you bring it back. That's an order."

Ever the soldier, Brian sat at his desk and went along with the joke that he could ever get all of this done by deadline. He glanced in the direction of surrounding co-workers, none of whom were looking at him, and made various faces that conveyed, "Ha-ha, funny joke, everyone. You sure stuck it to old Brian. You've pranked him good! Now I'll be a good sport and play along and sweat and moan as I frantically try to do the impossible."

Or maybe they weren't looking at him because he reminded them too much of mortality. He was the death row dog of the kennel. The once-in-a-lifetime ritual sacrifice of the no-kill shelter. Conspiracy in the anthill. Fed to the gods of contracts and bottom lines. The death in deadline. The canary in the coalmine of big accounts. The trafficked whore presented to the CEO to seal the deal.

Brian might have shocked the world and got a tremendous amount of work done that day if it hadn't been for the woman who recently returned from maternity leave. He didn't like her before. He really didn't like her now. All day she rambled on about "My baby this, my darling that". The Field Marshal even stopped by to chat with her. She never would have allowed him such galling lengths of brevity. His boss casually half-sat across the edge of the new mother's desk and jovially looked at snapshots on her screen. With each "Oh that's soooo cute!" she'd glance over at Brian as if to rub salt in his wounds. He was convinced she cared nothing for that baby and would probably feed it to her purebred dogs in a pinch. She was only using it as cover so she could watch him squirm. He was Lieutenant Suicide Mission and she was giggling on the sidelines of the trenches.

It would not have surprised Brian at all if she had rose and declared a spontaneous company picnic only to point out that Brian would unfortunately have to stay behind to work on the big account. But there was steel in Brian's gaze. He'd get work done just the same. He wouldn't let her win the war of wills.

"This woman would let the company fail just to see it blamed on me! So perverse is her vendetta against me that she has jeopardized an entire account by putting the work of ten people upon me! How can I win against such madness, such...*nihilism*?"

Brian brought to bear every ounce of his concentration to just. try. to. complete. one. line. And he broke. He lost. He glanced over. How could he not? The "tap tap tap" of her heel against the metal leg of the desk was her secret weapon, the nuclear option. From the morning upstairs stomps, to the construction jackhammer, to the demon hanging the placard in the lobby, the banshees had poisoned his every move. Now she sat there with that gleeful expression fooling every jackass in there that her joy was for the baby and not from gloating over his psychological torture.

The work day ended, but the ordeal carried on. Brian found himself post-microwave meal alone in his apartment staring at his desk. The huge clunky wooden desk that thumbed a nose at sleek, modern functionality beckoned Brian to sit. A particularly loud bang to the ceiling caused his teeth to clench. A car's headlights cast a spotlight moving beam across the walls. The transitioning light scanned Brian to find him now wearing the headphones, still standing there staring at the desk.

Data is the soul of the spreadsheet. The grid is the body. The endless numbers, equations, operands, arguments, the countless categories, words, designations and descriptions that fill the cells give it life. One misplaced figure can kill the patient; like a faulty valve a misplaced bit of data sends the system into seizures. Brian tries to think three cells ahead like a chess master, but renewed baby lead-foots to the ceiling cause him to lose the entire plot. The past hour of work flatlines in a code blue of distraction and shattered concentration. The spreadsheet is hemorrhaging. For reasons beyond his ability to comprehend, Brian sees the face of the Field Marshal hovering like a hologram within the monitor.

"Brian. Brian, you're losing your...patient! You're losing your...patience, Brian."

"Is she saying 'patient' or 'patience'?" he mutters to himself. She's saying neither because she's not there.

As the banging from above continues to overcome the defences of the headphones, Brian manages to look away from the screen and admire the desk instead. He can't so much hear the stomping as he can *feel it*. He could be completely deaf and he'd still feel the vibrations. He'd probably feel them even more.

Brian rose and tried to cross the room but each thump from the ceiling hammered his feet down into the floor. It was like quicksand. He managed to make it to the small dresser drawer by the door and pulled out a long black scarf. Like an invisible man revealing himself by wrapping bandages around his face, Brian did his best to encase his head in the wool garment. The reverberations bypassed his defences and came up through his feet. He grabbed two cushions from the small couch and placed them on the floor beneath the desk and rested his feet on them. His elbows and

Muffler

forearms felt the quivering of the chair. He put on a thick coat. He attempted the delicate work of properly populating the cells with all the freedom of a tightly bound mummy.

While his right hand threatened to crush the mouse, his left began to caress and then squeeze the bulky top of the desk. The legs were large and long. The six drawers heavily buttressed with wood. A sea of grain. A stout back panel that came nearly down to the floor had the seriousness of a border fence. A Berlin Wall of the desk world. The wooden slab on top was thick like a butcher's block. Brian felt the urge to climb into one of the big drawers. After staring at it for an undetermined amount of time, he roughly shoved himself back from it as if in horror - no, not horror, *revelation*. It was like he was staring at a bland work of art that had suddenly revealed hidden layers of meaning. Salvation in the banal. Mercy in the mundane.

Brian grabbed his keys.

The now familiar parking lot of the hardware store was playing host to a small teenage hangout as Brian pulled up. As he exited his car, the greasy-headed teen leaning into the car two spots away turned to look at him.

"Oh, hey, dude. Come back for more ear plugs? What are you doing, blowing stuff up?" The young punk seemed more a simpleton than a jerk to Brian, but it didn't make him dislike the kid any less. The only response the clerk got was the sight of Brian lifting his chin in an unnatural upward motion while tightening the veins and tendons in his neck. Brian's head and neck looked like a crooked screw that had been forced into an inadequate hole and now an unseen force was trying to extricate it.

The young greaser said something to his buddies in the car and headed back in behind Brian. He let out a "Whoa, dude!" when Brian came to the counter carrying a saw, hammer, electric drill, bits and various screws. "Wow, you're getting serious, man. Going in for some major DIY, eh, bro?"

Brian stared at the youth as if he was looking at the poster child of all that had gone wrong in the world. It was as if this very kid, with his greasy hair hanging down in his face, was the Typhoid Mary of impending social collapse. He was ground zero for the death of ambition and good manners combined. Brian had the urge to complain to the store manager about the boy's uncalled for and overly familiar tone. The only thing that stopped him was the knowledge that the manager was going to be just as stupid and insufferable. Brian would end up having to interact with two dullards instead of just the one. Best to cut his losses and exit as quickly as possible.

Brian almost succeeded in walking away, but an invisible force stopped him, and he found himself saying to the clerk, "I have to repair what others have broken. I must build peace and quiet. I must construct a drawbridge that can then be raised to keep out the loud and the rude. You know *the rude,* don't you?" He paused, and for a moment looked at the teen instead of looking through him. "You know all about it. The uninvited conversations of an unwelcome guest. The cock-sure knowledge that everyone else wants to hear what you have to say no matter how...*annoying* it is."

The store was quiet aside from the insect buzzing of the fluorescent lights. Man with saw and hammer stood in oblique juxtaposition to slack-jawed boy and continued. "I have to change *everything* (again the utter pain) about my life because everyone else can't keep theirs under control. You sea of...*loudmouths* (pure hatred) so completely un-self-aware seek out any spot of peace and quiet like starving animals and devour it. If you find an empty box you must remove the lid and shout into it."

Brian's eyes lit up. He sensed the hideous beauty of his soliloquy.

Muffler

"Does it kill you? Does it kill you all to know that your clatter cannot penetrate outer space? That even if you all shout and cry and bang on drums that it will peter out once it runs out of atmosphere. You can run and *stomp on the floor* (near rage) all you want, but the heavens won't hear you!"

Brian felt flush. He could feel himself growing. He could feel himself becoming something else. It was like the spectacle of his true form had become visible at that moment. The pathetic teen run-at-the-mouth would try to describe the awe-inspiring sight to his stoner friends but it would all be lost on them, for every other word out of their mouths was "awesome" and they no longer had any context for the meaning of it.

"The dignified on this earth must expend constant energy retreating from the foul stench of bad manners. The one great offense (confidence of certitude) that the noble and self-possessed must still suffer is the sea of people who don't know their place and can't shut-up."

A calmness came over him. At that moment, Brian was sure that he was surrounded by white light.

"Great ideas and moments of transcendent peace never happen because they are ploughed under by the rakes and blades of peasants who see any fertile ground as a dumping zone for their mediocrity. If the secrets of life and wisdom were spoken they would be quickly drowned out by the belches and farts and insipid conversations of the chatty class. Silence is torture to the thing that must hide its stupidity behind noise."

Brian paused and appeared to realize that he could do no better than that and so turned to make a triumphant exit.

Brian was nearly to the door so might or might not have heard the teen clerk finally manage to say, "Dude, that was awesome!"

Once back home, Brian enjoyed a small bit of payback. With each stomp from above he reciprocated with hammer blows. With each vibration of the walls and floor, he sawed into the wood with increasing frenzy. The sweat dripping from his brow lubricated the teeth as the saw chewed through the desk. The second-generation habitual eye closer upstairs was tempted to rat him out to her landlord mom, but her phone was across the room and the couch had too firm a grip on her ass.

Even though he had no carpentry skills to speak of, Brian worked as if possessed. A long cut of the top and backrest was nearly enough. He only had to affix a foot's worth of material to make it work, and he easily achieved that by cannibalizing the drawers. But when he got to the sides he realised he was lacking necessary tools. His frustration was quelled by the landslide of an adrenaline dump. Kneeling with a saw in one hand and a clenched fist in the other, Brian looked around at the mess he had made of his apartment. Saw dust was everywhere. His once mighty oak desk was in pieces. His laptop sat untouched just a few feet from the construction zone. The infernal noise from above had abated. Brian's chin dropped to his chest, and he quietly sobbed.

He had known the old desk since childhood. It had belonged to his Grandfather. Everyone else in the family had thought his Grandfather was a bit of a nut, but Brian liked him. In fact, he was about the only one he liked. As a kid, Brian didn't need attention and affection, which was good, because his parents gave neither. His Grandfather didn't either, but at least he was interesting. He had all kinds of strange books and weird objects sitting around. Sometimes he'd talk about magic and show Brian some tricks right there on the big, wooden desk.

There was also a giant, black-lacquered cabinet against the wall. His Grandfather teased him that it was his "disappearing cabinet". If he needed to get away, all he had to do was climb in. Brian believed him for years. He wished he had that cabinet now, but he

Muffler

was lucky to have the desk. His parents had a falling out with his Grandfather and decided that he was "putting weird ideas" in Brian's head and no longer allowed him to go over. They were even threatening to put him in a home.

He died suddenly after Brian left for college. His parents wanted to get rid of everything, but Brian returned for a weekend, hired a van and hauled the desk back to school. The cabinet was already gone, and his mom claimed she knew nothing about it. He had to keep the desk in storage for over a year before he moved into a space large enough for it.

Now it lay in pieces on his floor.

Brian recalled standing in his Grandfather's empty house and staring at the huge black cabinet. For a moment, he had felt convinced that his Grandfather wasn't dead but had merely stepped inside. It was the last time Brian had wept, until now.

When he walked into the office the next day he felt covered in gauze. The one or two greetings from disinterested co-workers sounded like garbled voices over a shortwave radio. The only comfort he found was by handling the small bits of wood he had in his sport coat pocket. After he had destroyed the much-loved desk (and ceased sobbing), he sat quietly on the carpet and chiselled and sawed off a few bits of wood in various shapes and sizes. He sat down slowly at his desk and ran his hands outward over the top like he was unrolling a blueprint. He caressed the edges and felt down the sides like he was touching a woman's shoulders. He ogled the desk as if to guess her dimensions. Did she have any useful parts to scavenge?

While his computer booted, Brian fiddled with the small bits of wood from his pocket. He was trying to piece them together or at least visualize a plan. He managed to assemble the little bits into a tiny mock-up of his project, but it wouldn't stay together. With deep concentration, Brian snipped off tiny lengths of a paperclip with scissors. He then held the metal filaments down with one blade of the scissors and bent the wire up so it made an angle. After a quick visit to the office supply cupboard, he put minute drops of glue on the tiny maquette and pressed the bent little wires in place. His concentration was broken by the voice of the Field Marshal. Brian had been so deep in thought that even he had not heard the clacking of her heels on the tile.

"Gooood morning, Brian!" she said with a nauseating mixture of saccharin and spite. "I'm *sure* I don't have to remind you that next week is the deadline and I'm *sure* you haven't made any plans this weekend since I'm *sure* you'll be busy putting some last-minute polish on your report. This one means *everything* to us Brian. This one could make or break us!" She laid a skeletal hand on his shoulder that still managed to have a grip of steel. "And I'm *sure* you know that if we break, some...*parts* will have to be *replaced*. Right, Brian?"

Just when he thought she was going to leave, she said, "And what exactly is that thing you're hiding in your hand? I'd say distraction is our number one enemy right now."

He froze and had a flashback to his mother always doing the same thing – trying to pry into everything, searching his room or finding a book on magic given to him by his grandfather. "Brian, you know you're not allowed to have this kind of evil trash in this house!" And with that he never got to finish reading about how a "disappearing cabinet" or anything else worked. Bobbie's voice broke him out of his time-traveling trance.

"You know, the more I think about it, distraction is like the naughty twin of concentration. When distraction enters the room, concentration goes out the window." She seemed very satisfied with that. "Yes, concentration goes out the window..." she trailed off as she appeared ready to relent and head back to her office. Her sudden urge to go write down her latest "witticism" saved Brian from any further humiliation. But then, at the last minute, she did the unthinkable and took her putrid hand from his shoulder and just barely touched the side of her burnt stick of a finger against the edge of his jaw.

Brian was sure her hands, her skin automatically attracted anything foul. He just knew he had a streak of germs along his jawline, if not outright fecal matter. A nearly invisible smear of noxious bacteria was already radiating out towards his mouth. He closed his eyes and could see an ultraviolet light being held up to his face. It revealed a wriggling mass of insectoid infestation. She had diseased him. If she couldn't stress his way into the hospital, she would give him the plague. While one or two of his co-workers would attend his funeral out of some vague sense of obligation, she would sit at her desk grinning as she erased his name from the big final report. She would be promoted with a raise and juicy bonus. She'd see fit to have a lackey send fifteen-dollars' worth of flowers to his grave as proof of how compassionate she was.

Brian stumbled to the toilet with the "infected" side of his face tilted up in a state of near-rigor mortis. He stood in the sickly urine-yellow light and scrubbed at it. Before he could adequately treat the wound, piss-shuffler Rich came in and mounted the urinal. As Brian tried to clean his face, the obscene grunts and motions of his co-worker kicked up more filth to pollute his flesh. There was no escaping contagion. They would infiltrate your eyeballs with their ugly and ridiculous faces. They would molest your ears with obscene noises not even heard among the lowest of barn animals. And then in all their gall, they would even reach out and touch your face. Fresh from the depths of their ghastly orifices, their filthy phalanges would smear their shame onto you like rancid butter. It was worse than being the last man alive in a sea of zombies. At least zombies would have the decency to kill and consume you. This lot, as if sensing you are the last righteous one remaining, commits itself to taunting and corrupting everything.

In his frantic haste to wash the side of his face, jaw, and neck Brian had gotten his collar wet. As he tried in vain to dab it dry, the urinal vulgarian mounted the sink with the same grotesque posture he assumed at the pisser. He then let out something that sounded like an "uhm, hmmm" as if he needed to announce himself to the sink and mirror each time he approached. This was the kind of guy who wasn't content with simply ruining a situation with his mere presence. No, he would have to narrate it as well. If he pinched your arm he'd surely accompany it with "I'm pinching your arm. I'm pinching your arm".

"Mmm, uhhh," he exhaled out of his gross, fish-like mouth.

Brian froze and took on a nauseated expression as he came to the realization that the guy wasn't going to wash his hands. He just brushed his thinning hair back and wiped a finger under his nose while sniffling. An uncomfortable amount of time had likely passed before Brian realized that the guy was matching his gaze in the mirror.

"What happened? Did you miss your mouth?" asked the disgusting co-worker.

"What?" responded a stupefied Brian.

"Did you try to take a drink and water your shirt instead?" Suddenly this vulgar shit had turned the tables on Brian and made *him* the butt of ridicule.

"Uh, no!" was the only retort Brian could muster. Well, that and the physical recoil of his torso away from the offending, impudent co-worker.

"Ha, ha! I'm just messin' with ya', buddy!" and with that the guy took his right hand - the same hand he had run through his lice-infested scalp and greased along the snotline of his upper lip - he took that very hand and slapped it down hard on Brian's shoulder and gave it a squeeze. The very same hand that had just been used to do you know what. As the contaminated, fleshy appendage withdrew, it performed a disdainful wiping motion along the fabric of his dress shirt.

Brian tried to continue dabbing at his wet collar, but his hand was shaking uncontrollably. Eventually some semblance of him staggered out of the men's room. Brian must have looked a bit odd with his right arm curled up unnaturally along his torso. His pale, trembling fingers tried to gingerly push the damp shirt collar away from his neck. The more it touched his skin the more he envisioned that vulgar co-worker wiping his wet hands all over him. The spongy material pawed at him like a smelly, rain-soaked dog.

Brian's body nearly went diagonal when he diverted towards the exit. He blew through the double doors leading into the lobby, zoomed past the elevator and nearly launched himself through the door to the stairwell. He made it two flights down before he realized he didn't know where he was going or what he was doing. A non-descript door that didn't look like all the others beckoned him. He didn't expect it to open, but it did. Brian found himself in what appeared to be some sort of narrow service corridor. It was lit only by a couple yellow lights spaced along a peeling wall. It was warmer and felt drier back there. That alone was reason to forge on. The corridor ended. Brian jerked his head around overcome by the sensation he had been followed and was now trapped. No one. But there was a door. Another door to his left. It was the same color as the walls and if not for the tarnished metal doorknob might have gone unnoticed. He turned the knob. He was sucked in.

The upward rush of air was disorienting. For a moment, he feared he had stepped right into the abyss, but a look down revealed a metal grate walkway. The roar was pleasantly deafening. Best of all, the constant flow of air was drying his collar. He had, as if by providence, found the HVAC area of the entire building. Brian leaned over the rail and let the rush of warm, dry air sanitize and encase him. His wispy hair wildly danced upward, and the warmth calmed him. All the noise and the filth was safely sealed out behind him. He cared not if this air was dirty. Brian wasn't some kind of clean freak, thank you very much. He was not concerned for his hearing either as the system roared. This was pleasant noise. This was nothing. Dust or dirt against which he held no grudge. It was them. It was *that filth* that had the gall to touch him. Brian raised his arms into the turbulent air triumphant.

But then Brian's refuge was jeapordized by a sweep of light. Even though he didn't hear it, the change in room pressure alone confirmed that someone had opened the door. As it turned out, anyone would have been better than the specter he feared. In his head, it was the Field Marshal standing there. She very well may have had a tracking device on him. So it was with a sense of relief that Brian turned and saw that it was instead some thin faced man with a shock of greasy black hair spilling back from a receding hairline. The apprehension on the intruder's face was softened by the slow, purposeful rubbing of a dirty cloth between his hands.

"What'cha doin' here, buddy?" asked the guy who looked like a gas station attendant who had escaped from a black and white 1950s film noir.

"I work upstairs. I got turned around," Brian replied as innocently as possible.

"Hard to get so turned around as to make your way all the way back here," said the greaser with an odd, evolving grin coming over his face.

The guy illustrated the fact that he didn't really care what Brian's reason was for being there by carrying on and not waiting for an answer. "Peaceful in here, ain't it?" The grin got bigger. "Not even my supervisor comes back here. Only ones that might is if there's some work being done. But that don't happen too often."

Muffler

"You wanna see some more? You might as well since you're down here," said Brian's new little friend. Again, the phantom of the HVAC opera didn't wait for a response and instead motioned with his already crooked head towards the right where the metal grated walkway nearly disappeared into blackness. Brian followed.

There were two steps down and a few steps forward until a wall appeared to the left and separated them off from the multi-floor air tunnel that rose from basement to roof. They went through a door and down a few more steps. It was all barely lit by weak, grey light. Finally, Igor wrenched open a metal door that looked like it had led a long life of routine abuse. The room was so dark the entrance was a rectangle of black ink.

His guide found the switch and illuminated the space with the familiar grey cast. There were shelves everywhere, on racks, assembled or stacked on the floor. Boxes limp with oil stains lined what might have passed as a walkway. "There's stuff been here lots longer than me," said the man as he glided along with his hand caressing the air just above all the clutter.

The two of them stood in silence. Then almost out of the embarrassment of two grown men finding themselves enjoying a place, a thing, a sensation that hardly anyone else would, Brian's guide blurted, "Well, anyway, it sure seems weird to be in such a place as this knowing that just out there (motioning out at the rest of the building surrounding them) there's all those folks running around in them there offices being so serious, worried about what comes next in that stressful business world all dressed up in their suits and ties and what-not."

A pause of indeterminate length.

"They don't know what's coming next." But then as if he too realized how creepy that sounded, he quickly added with a grin, "But I guess none of us do, eh, buddy?"

Muffler

If there had been any discomfort on Brian's part, it was dispelled by the presence of a stack of metal parts in a box to his left. He reached down and pulled one out. It was a bracket of some sort with a 90-degree bend.

"You interested in that?" asked the dude who looked like he sneaked around a lot.

"Are there more?" Brian asked.

"Oh yeah, I think there's quite a few more in there." Igor craned his neck. Curiosity got the better of him, "what'cha gonna do with 'em? You gonna build something?"

"Yes. I'm building something."

"Something important?"

"Yep."

"Is it big?"

"Not too big."

A spell of silence.

"Is it for yourself?"

"Huh? Yeah, just for me. Why do you ask?"

"Oh, I didn't know if you was making something to sell maybe."

"No, not to sell."

"Oh well then, I guess you can just have a few if you really need them."

"Oh, thanks. That would be great."

The hermit of the Heating, Ventilation and Air Conditioning cave watched over Brian as he rummaged through the boxes. There was a hint of pride or satisfaction on his face as if he was wondering if Brian knew how lucky he was. If this lost businessman did indeed realize how fortunate he was to get to walk out with some souvenirs then the bond was real. If he didn't get it, then well, the mysteries of the place were his to keep, and the separation from the surrounding world remained intact. He couldn't have a bunch of them starting to show up and ruin things. Before you knew it, there'd be secretaries sneaking cigarettes or adulterous couples coming in to grope each other. But this guy seemed alright.

The man beamed when Brian stood up clutching around ten good looking brackets. Dusty and a bit rusty, but imbued with the strength that comes from longevity.

"For all we know, those things are left over from the old factory that stood here before its shell was converted into this here office block." Old Tommy toolbox remembered the place from when he was a kid. He and his pals used to ride their bikes around it, peer inside the smashed windows and try to scare each other with made-up tales about the place. One kid had sworn that his grand daddy had died in the place. And now the dark innards of the office building were all that remained of that past. The metal bits and some scattered old tools were like the contents of a time capsule. Progress and plastic would form around it, but this chamber remained. The old days hung in the air. Down in the sub-basement a section of stone wall remained that was clearly older than everything else. A portion of the floor down there was hard, compressed dirt, and it smelled different than everything else - like oil, sweat, hard work and ghosts.

He knew letting Brian take those things wouldn't dent the legacy one lick. If anything, it was good to see a few of the relics go back into use. That was their intended function after all, to be used, to hold something together. Whether he forgot he already had asked or was just trying his luck again, the maintenance man of recent antiquities looked at Brian and asked, "What'cha building?"

This time (if it was indeed a second time) Brian answered.

"A box."

The widow-peaked head of the maintenance man glowed in the industrial-shop grey light as he eyed Brian. His deadpan face slowly transformed with a grin. "A box, huh? Good. That's good. Hold some stuff inside."

Brian returned to realizing how strange the whole situation was when the skinny old guy wearing the generic blue-colors-of-work-clothes-everywhere held out his hands towards Brian and acted like he was shifting air at him and remarked, "Here, put some of this old air in the box."

The old guy's laughter echoed behind him as Brian stumbled out the way he'd came. As he made his way back along the metal grate hovering above the great abyss he dropped one of the brackets. It clanged loudly against the metal but did not fall through. As he gingerly knelt to retrieve it, a voice drifted across the expanse. "Maybe it don't wanna go!" More laughter followed down the grey-green corridor. Brian leaned heavily against the left wall. He suddenly felt out-of-sorts as he faced the transition back into the real world. The heavy-glassed industrial lighting protected beneath metal cages illuminated his gaunt face as he half-slid himself along the wall clutching the brackets. His barely free right hand fumbled for the knob. The usually dim lighting of the stairwell was now blinding.

Brian knew he couldn't take the old brackets into his office. If Field Marshal Bobbie saw them, she'd fixate on them and ask too many questions. She'd probably accuse him of stealing. It dawned on him that he was technically stealing since that strange guy lurking in the ventilation system probably didn't have the authority to give him anything from the building. In his head, Brian saw a series of events unfold where the Marshal would demand to confront this person who supposedly gave the parts to him. In desperation to keep his job, Brian would take her down there, but then the guy would be nowhere to be found. No one would have even heard of him. Hell, the space itself, the door, the corridor, none of it would be there and Brian would be left standing in the stairwell with the Marshal looming over him with folded arms as he groped along the wall searching for the hidden door to the bowels of the building. By the time he'd turn around, she would have quickly gotten half of the office to come down and gawk at him. They'd be crowded on the landing and jostling on the stairs to get a look at him as he gesticulated around like a madman. Look at the freak, the lunatic, the poor slob who imagines phantoms roam the dark innards of a structure that is, in truth, just a soulless building in the middle of nowhere.

Brian was afraid she'd see him going to his car from her lair on the 5th floor. He'd turn to look and she'd slowly extend an accusative finger down at him. The thought of her having something on him caused his stomach to spasm. He held them close to his side and quickly went back up the flights of stairs. Inside the door leading off the 5th floor stairwell was the small entrance area. The elevator was there as well as a couple chairs and three fake plants. Two of them were in large pots. It was there that Brian made the last minute, nearly panicked decision to stash the brackets behind the one nearest to the stairwell. As he reached to open the beige metal door, his hands were sweating so bad that two of the brackets slipped from his left hand and clanged on the floor. In the crouching position, he just knew she was going to come through that door. She'd catch him there, sweat and rust and all.

"Why are you away from your desk, Brian? And why do you have those old brackets, Brian? Is your shabby little desk falling apart from all the sweat you drip on it as you worry about whether you're up for the job? ANY job?"

But his luck was still holding as he managed to gather the brackets and make it into the foyer. As quick as he could, he stashed the brackets behind the large planter. He was confident no one would look back there - not today at least. And even if they did, so what? They couldn't pin the brackets on him. What proof would they have? As he reached to open the door into the office, he noticed the rust stains on his hands; stains as red as blood.

Brian did his best invisible man routine and slinked through the door and then directly into the men's room where he washed away the evidence the best he could. Upon exit, his eyes did the Field Marshal radar sweep that he had perfected over the years. The coast was clear, and he made it back to his desk unmolested. There was still some time to get a chunk of work done before the weekend. He knew he couldn't count on getting much done at home, not when the bastards would inevitably be causing a racket.

Brian sucked in air and pulled himself back from anger. He remembered that it hadn't been such a bad day after all. That area downstairs, the ventilation catacomb, it had refreshed him, and he found the brackets! His eyes dared to look in the general direction where they were hidden. If he got a lot done this afternoon he'd have ample time for his project at home.

"Yes. Determination," he thought to himself. "Get this stuff done!"

Not thirty seconds into his spreadsheets, Brian's attention was drawn to a sudden figure. There was no denying it. It was him. Bruce. Bruce the idiot janitor with his thick glasses and dumb expression and 1950s style haircut. He was a mouth-breather but an efficient cleaner. "Too god damned efficient!" Brian clenched his teeth. He knew there was no sense fixating on it, and that he needed to just get back to his spreadsheets. It's a Friday and even dull Bruce will be cutting corners to get out a minute early. Brian stared at his screen with determination. But then he acted like he needed to relieve his back by rising a bit up off the chair. That way he could get a look over the divider at the snoopy janitor. That's what he really hated about guys like him; just because they clean an area that makes them think they have some rights or authority over it. If slack-jawed Bruce looks behind that plant and sees those brackets he's just the type to run them straight into the Field Marshal and be all, "Look at me! I found something where it doesn't belong, and I'm bringing it to you the way a dog brings a dead squirrel to its master." And she'll look at him with scorn that's tempered with appreciation for his boot-licking. A fucking dumbass boot licker who will spoil Brian's one little victory of the day. She'll pat the toilet cleaner on the head and send him off with the brackets. Bruce the Victorious will solemnly place them in his regal janitor's closet where, god forbid, no one else can go. They'll go from being Brian's last magnificent pieces of the puzzle to worthless pieces of shit in the hands of the dullard. Day after day, he'll spend his breaks in that chemical smelling closet fawning and petting his discovered booty - his seized contraband like Gollum stroking his "precious". Meanwhile the project falls apart and old Brian loses AGAIN!

"Bullshit!" even with his teeth clenched like a paper shredder, the guy in the next cubicle looks over at him. And now HE knows that Brian is stressed about the janitor and now if the mopey mop-head finds the brackets, this nosey shitass will suddenly become Sherlock fucking Holmes and put two and two together. He'll observe the commotion being caused by the cleaner discovering the brackets. He'll then look over at me and slowly nod his head. Oh, bravo, genius, you figured it out!

Brian could just see him getting up and going over to the newly formed cabal and whispering to Bobbie. The coke-bottle glasses stool pigeon grasping his mop handle like a flagpole will crane his neck to see who the suspect is.

"As if he deserves to be among the first to ferret me out. The gall!" Brian winced when he couldn't be sure he didn't say it out loud.

Remembering how much work he still had to do on the big project, he tried to focus on his screen. He'd manage a minute or two of productivity but then fight the urge to turn to see where Bruce was. Finally, as if he could fool himself, Brian scrunched his shoulders and stretched his neck first to the right, as if to prove he wasn't giving in to the need to see where the janitor was, but then quickly swung back to the left, all the while dramatically exhaling like he was tired from working so hard. And when his chin went beyond parallel to his shoulder, Brian's eyes turned hard left as well. He looked just in time to see sneaky Bruce about to make his way out to the elevator lobby where Brian's treasure was hidden. Brian squeezed his mouse so hard the plastic on the sides cracked.

"Bastard," he hissed.

The water cooler was close to the lobby and Brian was suddenly very thirsty. He paced himself and snuck up to make sure the janitor didn't see him. He peered over the plastic cup from which he pretended to sip. He watched the janitor in his predictably no-nonsense blue uniform open the door and clumsily pull his canister vacuum behind him. The water resting against Brian's lip was joined by a bead of sweat. The python-like hose of the vacuum following its master.

"You sneaky little snake," thought Brian.

His gut twisted in knots when he realized the dolt was going to sweep the lobby. Brian could see it all. He'd snake that nozzle behind the planter and feel it bump against some foreign object. Then he'd stretch his serpent neck back towards the corner and find the brackets. Brian would still be standing there when he'd burst through the door with them. Brian could see it all. The Marshal wouldn't even need the help of the Sherlock sitting across from him. She'd march right out and find Brian still standing there at the cooler. Oh, he'd do his best to appear nonchalant, but she'd zero right in on him. It didn't fucking matter to her whether he was responsible for them or not! She'd WANT to pin it so badly on him that it would be a kangaroo court right there on the spot. Or, no, wait. Knowing her, she'd be right on the verge of confronting him but would then remember that the project is due, and her devious little brain would get to calculating and decide to just stare at him and take the contraband back into her office for another day. She'd wait until he handed in his (unfairly large) part of the work, give him a phony "thank you", and right as he was about to exit her office she'd say, "Oh, Brian, one other thing." He'd turn to see her pulling the brackets out of a desk drawer. "You know anything about these?" She will probably manage some intel between now and then and will have some circumstantial evidence that connects him. Maybe she'll have the maintenance guy in the catacomb questioned and he'll spill the beans. Hell, he'll most likely cover his own ass and say that he only saw Brian exiting the area with something in his hand. He won't even admit he gave Brian permission to take them! Hell, maybe that's what the son of a bitch does. He finds someone in the building to "give" something to and then denies it when his victim is found out. "What kind of loser gets his cheap thrills that way?!" Brian hissed through his teeth.

Brian knew he had to get it together as he felt full panic approaching. He was seconds away from losing those brackets and at best, his home project being severely set back. He'd have to go back to that hardware store and deal with that dreadful kid. There'd be more sophomoric questions about what he was up to. Besides, brand new, heavy-duty brackets like that probably cost a fortune.

"Why can't I get something free and easy for a fucking change?"

In a clutch move, Brian zipped back to his desk and grabbed some data print-out and quickly, but unsuspiciously, made his way towards the lobby. He formulated the plan as he went. "Improvisation," he thought to himself, "that's how I'll out-smart these fucks."

By the time he reached the door, he had it sorted. He'd play it off as a move to concentrate. Go for the "intensity" angle. Walk it off to get it right. Peripatetic solutions to pressing problems. That way, if she came out, he'd have a reason to be pacing in the lobby. It would seem an odd place to concentrate, what with the roar of the vacuum, and she'd surely bring that up. Yes, he'd retort that it was a counter-intuitive thing for him. That the noise helped him. It is, white noise after all, so why not? Just then, the janitor would turn to see what the ruckus was all about and then spot the brackets. BAMM. Brian's right there for convoluted reasons acting strange, giving oblique responses to simple things right as Swifty the Sweeper yanks out the brackets. Might as well be fucking bones. Might as well be a corpse being discovered in Brian's backyard by a nosey cop who just happened to wander by. Busted. On the spot. No escape. No retreat. But it was too late to back out, and Brian passed through the door.

Bruce was over in the far corner about to sweep around to the right in the direction of the planters. He'd at least have to get past the chair that sat in front of the plant. Brian stared intently at the papers and headed quickly towards ground zero. The janitor whipped the vacuum extension around so quick that Brian barely beat him to the spot. He continued to pretend the cleaner wasn't there. Bruce waited thinking Brian was going to go out the far door, but he just stood there.

Finally, Brian glanced up at him and improvised his best "Oh, hello, don't mind me" accompanied by a half-hearted waving gesture and plopped down in the chair. He then leaned forward and studied the paper as if the fate of the world depended on it. But he wasn't looking at the paper at all but peering under it. The scratched metallic edge of the vacuum attachment came ever closer to his foot. It would move in then back off. In and out. Back and forth. Brian seriously doubted that a piece of cardboard would have fit between the tip of his shoe and the vacuum as the jerk janitor pushed his luck. When it withdrew, Brian braced himself, convinced that the next sortie would deliberately ram his shoe like a kamikaze pilot.

"Who IS this shit who thinks that sweeping the damn carpet is more important than me, a proper employee here with serious work at hand trying to concentrate? Millions of dollars are riding on what I'm doing, and he's inconvenienced because I'm keeping him from vacuuming a couple square feet of carpet!"

Brian's neck and chin contorted with disgust at the obscene lack of respect and perspective in the world. If this jackass worked at a hospital, he'd block a stretcher with a mangled car crash victim on it just so he could mop a square tile. He'd be canned from any film set because he'd repeatedly stick his mug in the shot to dust off the boom mic. A scientist could be a step away from curing cancer and this pathetic shit would knock over the test tubes while wiping the table. The ink of a poet's magnum opus would run down the page as janitor-boy drips caustic cleaning solution over it.

Brian bolted up. He did the hand-close-to-face gesture as if in maximum concentration. He stood like an obelisk blocking the raider from the treasure. The low-life would have to thrust the vacuum between Brian's legs if he wanted to get to the area behind the planter.

"He better not dare."

Right as the peasant appeared to signal defeat by withdrawing his hose-tethered forces, it happened; she came through the door.

Brian's blood turned to thorns and scratched at his insides. He excitedly jabbed at the paper as if he was right then solving everything. So deep in professional contemplation was he, that he had no idea she was even there. Surely, even she would respect such intensity and move on. Maybe if he *became the paper* she wouldn't even see him. His eyes turned to branding irons. This was it. The worst-case scenario was about to happen. She was going to accost him and then spot the brackets. Snuffy Smith there would guffaw at him for getting emasculated. He even shut off the vacuum as soon as the Field Marshal entered. It's plaintive call slowly trailing off until the silence in the lobby was painful.

He lost. Brian lost the non-staring contest. His eyeballs jerked up like they were yanked by fish hooks. She met his gaze.

"For god's sake, Brian, get out of the man's way so he can do his job!" she moaned at him as she turned to summon the lift.

Just when he thought the doors were safely sealing her in, she stabbed her wooden finger at the buttons and held open the door. "Oh, Brian, I assume I don't need to remind you that I'm going to need to see all your completed work in my office first thing Monday morning. STAT. The client's coming in on Wednesday so I'll have a couple days to hopefully catch any mistakes you've made." She almost let go of the door-open button, but instead he could sense her digging her finger into it even deeper. "Don't disappoint me, Brian. Remember, no excuses, no compromises!" And with that the button exhaled, relieved to be free of her greasy, scaly skin.

The doors came together like a tomb being sealed. The evil countenance of the Pharaoh queen glaring at him until the very end.

Bruce the janitor waited patiently for Brian to glance at him, then gave him a championship smirk.

With the Marshal out of the office and the janitor heading off to his closet lair, Brian grabbed the chance to retrieve and shove the brackets into a plastic bag he scavenged from the breakroom. He then quickly marched them back to his desk and stowed them in his insulated lunch box. At the end of the day, he once again feigned deep concentration while looking at print-outs to discourage anyone from engaging him as he headed for the stairs. Once he made it safely to his car, he felt a rare sense of relief, almost euphoria. Maybe things would be okay after all.

Brian did his best to enjoy his dinner. Beside the microwave lasagne meal were three florets of broccoli and two cherry tomatoes. It was a fresh veg full-hand. He always made sure to eat one of the healthy things first. He didn't mind broccoli, but let's face it, it pales in comparison to the salty, fatty, squishiness of the processed lasagne. He would leave the last, sweet tomato to signal the end of the meal. It's tart freshness a small way to cleanse the palate of the guilt of the other, calorie rich fare.

He was just about to reach for that solitary little tomato when it quivered. It quivered again. His chin and neck did that spasm thing that made it look as though he was attempting to retract his face into the back of his skull. The Horror Above reminded him of all the work his project still required.

He could only pause and question his sanity when he walked into the living room and saw the old wood desk scattered around the floor in pieces. Tools and sawdust formed a maze to navigate. He had nowhere to work. Any thoughts of working at the kitchen table or on the floor were aborted by the near-continuous noise from above. There was a good reason his desk was in pieces. It was now incumbent upon him to make something important out of it. It was the last trace of his Grandfather upon the earth, and it could now very well prove to be Brian's salvation.

His spirits were lifted when he remembered his booty. He hurried over to his lunch kit and anxiously unzipped it. Out spilled a pile of tarnished and rusty brackets. All those ninety-degree angles looked reassuring, like you could build a whole room with them or a square cocoon. He fingered them as if inspecting for flaws or to appreciate each one's unique patina. So well-worn yet capable.

With a drill and some wood screws, he began to assemble sides to the base. In some places two pieces of the desk had to be spliced together to make up the right size. Such was the case with the top. The largest remaining length of wood was only chest high. Brian had to splice another section on to it. He didn't have the time or supplies to glue the two pieces together. The brackets were all he had. Even though they bent at a 90-degree angle, there were screw holes at both ends of each metal arm, that way he was able to span the rough line where the desk pieces met and stitch them together like a wound. The end product looked odd, but serviceable. He had used two brackets, and the unused perpendicular part stuck up off the lid like spikes. If anything, they gave the added bonus of providing an alternative grip for moving the heavy slab of sutured timber around.

Brian's satisfaction with his project was interrupted by a terrifying new sound. It was actually a quick series of sounds. No, it couldn't be. The usual plodding steps of the clay-footed toddler had given way to something else. "Thump thump thump" followed by the unmistakable sound of nails. Toe nails. Toe nails on faux wooden floors. More scratching along with vibrations. And that...that there - that was a jangle - the jangle of a collar. Laughter. Pounding. Thump thump thump. Scratching. Trotting. Slobbering. Jangling. Barking. Testing. Patience.

Brian's eyes bulged. The obviousness of the insult. The gall! It was as if every step he took to secure some peace was being tripped up in real time by the tormentors. Soon, every time he'd inhale they'd find a way to disperse noxious gas. Every ounce of sleep invaded by a nightmare. With each piss a burning pain. That's how deep this lot had gotten into his life. These bastards might all be in it together! A complex cruel hoax. Somewhere these evil shits meet, like a club. They probably find each other on the internet via their shared interests in finding undeserving people to torment. They go out for drinks and laugh it up as they try to outdo one another. Who can come up with the most insidious way to drive old Brian to an early grave? It surely gives them sick kicks and a sense of superiority since only they are in on the joke. Like they're some sort of fucking puppet masters pulling the strings of Brian's discontent. Amateur secret agents enacting an elaborate plan simply to drive some guy crazy.

"These pathetic shits are so terrified at the lameness of their own lives that they can get relief only by tormenting someone like me - someone who's better than them and exposes how sad they are. Not only that, but they need to make it a protracted game to truly get their thrills." With that, Brian's chin and neck made that increasingly frequent contortion that looked like a snake recoiling.

This time it sounded like the ball had been thrown against a wall as Brian's shrinking apartment reverberated. There was no denying it. The filth upstairs had gotten a dog and they were all mouth-drooling idiots now watching the dog scratch and pounce its way across the floor in pursuit of a ball. The monstrous little child clapping and running after it. It's club-feet doubling the steps of the dog. Amplitude multiplying. The dog's claws on the floor like fingernails on a chalkboard - all with laughs and screams.

By the time Brian finished his project the noise had abated and the sun set. He still had to test the fit. With a nod of accomplishment, he laid down in the oblong box and pulled the heavy lid closed. It was dark, but the rough cuts and seams here and there let in some of the artificial light from the room. The small gaps would also allow some fresh air, though he was quick to realize that perhaps he needed to drill a few holes here and there to ensure comfort.

After a bit more work, Brian seemed satisfied. Since it was just lying flat on the floor, it wasn't too hard to get in. But since he was no craftsmen, he'd have to be careful to not put too much pressure on the sides when climbing in and out. Once he was safely back in, his satisfaction was blanched by the realization that it wouldn't be easy to actually get any work done in the box. Could he have gotten this far only to see his dream run aground on the rocks of a practicality?

When Brian climbed out, he was startled to see that it was past midnight. The moon hung high in the sky and illuminated his room in a comforting, eerie blue glow. Upstairs the mother of the foot-stomping thing shifted in her bed. The distant whirring noise of Brian's drill wasn't quite loud enough to wake her. Of course, he couldn't care less if it did. Brian swept away the sawdust with a brush of his hand. With the help of some hook and loop and duct tape he chanced a solution.

The fly's view from the ceiling saw the lid being yanked back into place. The box sealed. Around the head it emitted a dim glow. The seam sutured with rusty brackets let out a slit of photons that fanned out towards the ceiling. Inside the prone occupant glowed like a pilot in a cockpit. All systems go. With elbows at his sides and forearms bent back he could manipulate the keypad. But it was late, and his hours of hard labor caught up with him. With the moon-like aura of the laptop screen illuminating his face, Brian fell asleep.

A few minutes into slumber and the screensaver kicked in. One thousand tiny stars sped endlessly across the screen. Arms folded and in deep slumber, Brian had the best sleep he'd had in ages.

For a brief, merciful moment Brian eased out of slumber without knowing why. But as soon as his brain was awake enough to know, his jaw clenched at the unmistakeable sounds and rumbling from above. His box repelled most of it, but the vibrations came up through the floor and disturbed the bottom of the box. The spot where the back of his head contacted the board buzzed with every stomp or bouncing ball from above. One was so heavy it jarred his laptop out of sleep mode. There in front of Brian was a highly incomplete spreadsheet.

It was tricky to remove the lid without knocking the laptop. The delicate manoeuvre made harder by the harsh blast of light that entered once Brian managed to lift the lid and move it aside. With eyes barely open, he sat up while guiding the heavy lid to the left until it rested partly on the floor and half against the box. Afraid to lift himself solely by pushing down on the edges of the two side walls, he had to get up a few moves at a time. Finally, he stepped out of the container and headed for the coffee machine.

Stiff and still a bit sleepy, Brian did a rickety dance into the kitchenette. It wasn't until after a few sips perked him up that he was able to turn back around and see his creation more clearly. In the cold light of day, it was a bit...*revealing*. Brian's face twitched at the now recognizable form of the oblong box. Even though his living room resembled a funeral parlour, he brushed it off, confident in the knowledge that necessity overrules decor.

Brian knew that time was running out. It should have been his Saturday to do as he pleased, but the amount of work he absolutely had to complete by Monday negated any notion of a weekend. But the ball was still bouncing. The feet still stomping. He climbed back inside his box and tried to enter the formulas in the right cells that would make sense of the mountains of data in his care. The thumps vibrated his head. He typed harder only to have to go back and correct mistakes. Right on the verge of discovering where he had gone wrong, an egregiously loud bang from above shattered his concentration.

Brian slid the lid off his container with such force that the shock caused his laptop to reboot. He lost several minutes of work. Not to worry. He could handle this. He retrieved his ear protection headphones and climbed back in and tried to recall where he had left off. All the sounds were well muffled, but the vibrations still found him. "Carry on, old boy, don't let the bastards win." But for the moment they did. Despite his mounting anger he was more careful in extracting himself this time. He ferreted out his large wool scarf and found a thick blanket to lay down in the bottom of the box. He was eager to try it out again, but his stomach was rumbling. He figured he might as well eat before he continued. Despite being physically hungry, his appetite was anaemic. All he could bring himself to prepare were some beans and toast. It took him a minute before he realized it was quiet. Maybe he'd get some work done without the need of his contraption after all.

Brian placed his plate in the sink and then removed his laptop from the underside of the lid. He looked around realizing he really didn't have a decent place to work since he had cut his desk into pieces. "Oh well," he shrugged to himself and plopped down on the floor, "this will do." As soon as he focused in on his work the ball bounced along the floor above him. Jaw clenched. Stomping feet. Veins popping out on neck and forehead.

"God-duh-duh-dammit!" Spittle ejected two feet ahead. Brian also made a strange whining noise that sounded like a high-pitched engine revving up "uhh-zeee!" as he drooped forward onto his knees and crawled towards the oblong box. He looked like a startled spider retreating into a burrow.

With the lid only halfway in place, he fumbled to attach the laptop. It fell and the top edge of the screen came down on his lip. "Ouch! Uhhh-zeeeee!" He sat up enough in the box to grab and swing the lid down onto the floor. It took every bit of restraint he had to not slam the laptop down onto it. Instead, he managed to gently put it in place where the Velcro straps came out of the crudely drilled holes. But he had to lean far out of the box to secure the right end of the laptop, causing the whole box to tip on its side spilling him onto the floor and planting his face yet again onto the laptop. "Bluh-zeeeeee!" he sputtered in a rage as he squirmed like a landed fish trying to right himself.

Brian scrambled to his feet and nearly fell again as he staggered to the bathroom to wash the spittle off his face and try to regain his composure. Looking at himself in the mirror he saw that the laptop keyboard had imprinted a row and a half of small, square indentations on his forehead.

"Uh, what's it spell, 'loser' on my head? You all think that would be funny, don't you?" Brian clutched the sides of the sink panting, trying to steady himself. He splashed a few handfuls of water on his face and used a towel to rub out the indentations. Bags under his eyes. Face drawn. Stubble. He looked like hell.

The noise from above was constant. Outside cars honked their horns. People spoke loudly on the sidewalks. Back in the front room and breathing hard, Brian squatted beside the lid and properly secured the laptop. Once he was in the box, he almost tipped it over again trying to hoist the lid from the side into place. He managed to not fall out again and secured the heavy, makeshift door to his compartment. The thick blanket made it more comfortable. It was a bit of a struggle to get the headphones on and wrap the scarf around them, but he managed. Nearly mummified, he practiced breathing only through his nose. Finally, settled in, Brian concentrated on the spreadsheets.

"The SUM of F4 through F32 will then be referenced by…" "Thump thump thump WUMP!" followed closely by a wailing child and then a barking dog. The noise was still discernible enough to be distracting. Or was the simple knowledge that it was happening enough to unnerve him? Then the crying little beast stomped across the floor, and the vibrations penetrated the best of Brian's defences. Chain of thought shattered. Jaw clenched. Hands trembling. Even with the thick blanket below him, the box still quivered with every bang from above. It took herculean self-control to extract himself once again without breaking anything in the process.

He gathered up every pillow in the apartment including the cushions from the couch and shoved them beneath the box. When minute vibrations still tingled his skin he climbed out yet again. Brian tore his mattress from the frame and drug it into the front room. He stacked the cushions and pillows upon it and with great difficulty managed to place the oblong box on top of all of them. It was unstable and swayed side to side as he climbed back in. Lid sealed. Ear muffs applied. Scarf mummifying his head. A new noise. A jingle. A jangle. A barely audible sound.

The telephone.

As much as he wanted to ignore it, once he heard the answering machine engage Brian pulled his earmuffs off. There was no mistaking the annoying voice of the Field Marshal. "Brian? Brian, are you there? You better pick up. I need to..."

Brian didn't hear the rest as he gave into his baser instincts and attempted to scramble out of the box. In his haste, he forgot that he had stacked it on his mattress and a mountain of cushions. It was all very unstable, and as soon as he leaned to the left the whole box, lid and all, tumbled to the side and dumped him down. Much like the tormenting ball upstairs, Brian bounced off the cushions, briefly took flight and landed face first on top of the lid. The oblong box remained wrapped around his legs and followed right after him. The right edge of it slammed down on his back and then his head.

"Huh-zeeeee!" Brian wheezed in pain and frustration as he worked to free himself from under the heavy container. When he tried to crawl towards the phone, the box stayed hooked on his heel and dragged behind him like a ball and chain. Dizzy and with trembling hand, Brian reached out towards the phone as the Field Marshal uttered a threat, a command to return her call within the hour and finished off with her signature move, "Remember, Brian, *no excuses, no compromises!*"

"Blurballabuh-duhduhduh." Brian emitted pathetic, incomprehensible noises as he crumpled flat on the floor. An observer might have thought he was having some sort of fit as he jerked and twisted to free his legs from the box. He crawled on all fours to tend to the mess scattered about the floor. The cushions had to be stacked back in place, and his back was so sore from being hit by the box that it caused great pain to try to heave it back on top and steady it in place. Brian almost tipped it all back over trying to get the lid back on.

Even though he finally made it back inside the protective cocoon, anyone of rational mind could see that the laptop had been severally damaged. Somehow it was still able to display a bluescreen, but it was cracked and flickered. Only someone on the inside could see the sad sight of Brian trying to make something happen by repeatedly pressing his fingers into the broken keyboard. Time passed; Brian lay motionless.

Another loud noise assaulted him. Someone was pounding at the door. His shoulders drew together. His rib cage retracted. Brian's eyes rolled up into his head as the sounds of the landlady shouting penetrated his box. The fact that she had the utter gall to be out there complaining about HIS noise caused Brian's joints to grind. The world had him cornered. There was only one way out and that was in.

The box had been only the beginning. With all his might, Brian withdrew a millimetre and then another and another. In the ever-so-slightly vacated space around him, he invokes his will to duplicate the box. Incrementally smaller, he encases himself like Russian nesting dolls. Shrivel and fortify. Shrink and barricade.

Muffler

The tomb of one thousand boxes battles the encroaching beasts in the war for Brian. Even as reprimands from the hall reach him, the stomping above continues as if they are now in all-out competition to see who finally breaks him. There is a slight pause and then the pounding resumes, this time in stereo. And on top of that, the blinky-eyed banshee is joined by an all too familiar voice. "Brian, this is your boss. You better be in there, Brian!"

"Brian. I need those reports. Brian, where are your spreadsheets?"

Brian presses the headphones so hard against his ears it feels like they are going to sink into his skull. He wills the box tighter. His soul retreats from the outside world like a fleeing army on the verge of being slaughtered. It's a matter of survival now.

The brackets tighten. The brackets curl. Those lovely, rusty brackets that he fought so hard for, mimic his contractions and squeeze in on the oblong box. The wood creaks under stress. He feels the sides pushing against his elbows. He feels his joints compress. And then he sees it. He sees the manual in his mind's eye. It is no trick. It is not something one can buy in a magic and joke shop. It must be created and willed. He knew it. He *knew* his Grandfather wasn't dead. He had figured it out too. No nursing home for him. No nagging, controlling voices at the end of his life. He had climbed into that magnificent, black lacquer cabinet and said the words and willed it so.

"To remove is to improve. Escape is my fate. No matter how many boxes they open, they will never reach me. No lid will give up my door. I am one step ahead. Even as their madness still reaches my ears, I shall simply disappear. Into this cabinet I go. Far away from everyone I know. You cannot have me. I blink, and now I am gone."

Darkness, quiet, solitude and void.

Muffler

Eventually, there is the sound of a key in the door. Bobbie stands outside, her high-heeled foot tapping in anticipation. "I really appreciate you letting me in. You have no idea how much trouble this joker has caused me."

"Oh, I'd believe it all right," said Brian's ever-blinking landlady, who now stared wide eyed into the room. "He's been nothing but trouble for me as well."

They entered the austere apartment together.

"Oh dear, what is all this sawdust doing here?" complained the landlady. "And all these cushions and a mattress! Does he have someone else sleeping here? I'll have to hire a cleaning crew to deal with this mess. I hope he doesn't expect to get his deposit back!"

"Well, he won't have a job soon, so get it while you can," Bobbie chimed in.

As they started to go, Bobbie saw a small object lying on the carpet almost covered in sawdust. For some reason she decided to scoop it up.

Back in her corner office, the odd little thing was placed near the right edge of her large desk. It was a miniature, crude, oblong box with tiny metal brackets at the corners. Bobbie wasn't sure why she liked it. If Brian ever had the nerve to show up again, maybe she'd show it to him just to let him know she had gone all the way into his home hunting him down.

At the end of one late night at work, she turned the lights off to her office, glanced back and could swear her little souvenir was glowing. Perhaps, one day she would try to open it up. But for now, it looked right at home next to the silver-plated placard she had custom made. She walked back over and slowly slid her finger along the little box and read aloud the slogan written in bold font upon the placard:

"No Excuses. No Compromises!"

Muffler

Artist by other name

Artist by Other Name

Artist by Other Name

Back in my country I work and like to make nice things from nature but then army men came and made life hard, dangerous. I wanted to stay, but momma beg me go. She say I be safe and earn money to send back, that I cannot help family if dead. I could not stand to say goodbye. In middle of night I left. I put note to family on table. Did not cry.

Hide during day and go at night. I make it to ocean. I pay what I had to get on boat. Very scary on the sea. So many people on boat. I try to sleep but only dream of drowning. I hear people cry and getting sick. I wish I be home. I get up and go to top. Sky is black and so many stars. Water and space look same. Like giant dark mouth of world. Feel like if I jump off I might not go in water but float off in space.

In morning I look back and old life gone. Night swallow it. Morning spit me out.

Finally boats come to us and give us jackets. We make it to the land. Happy and sad. Hopeful but afraid. Even ground feels different.

Life very different in Europe. Must learn language and strange ways. Very grateful. Life not in danger. Government people talk to me. I stay with many others in big building. Answer many questions. I am allowed to stay. Time goes by. Get job. Small flat with stove. Only two burners but it's enough to make meal. Bed is nice. Window. Sounds of city outside but no guns. Sleep good but sometimes wake and think of family.

Very good to get job with company. Not always easy to understand boss and instructions, but he is nice and will show me. I now know the word "scraper" and things like that. Stood by boss in station, he look around. Boss motion me over. Bend down. Use scraper to remove thing. Chewing gum. Sticky things on ground. I nod. Understand. Be at work early. Big train station always needs cleaned. Start at one end and by time get to the other need to start again. Soon day over. Cans, drinks, rubbish people leave. See red can next to green bench. Position is nice. Small child walk by and look to left. Make good picture, but must throw can away and move on.

Big job to keep things off floor. People spill drink and floor get sticky. I look at the floor all over. It is hard tile like rock. People don't notice it. It has nice patterns and how do you say...swirls? Different colors from one tile will go and change shape on next tile. This is like a mosaic.

In big train station many people come and go. Most nice. Most do not notice me. I sweep and pick up litter. Boss gives the scraper and tells me not to lose it. I know how to take good care of tools. Only had some things back home and had to treat them right so they last. "Do not worry," I say to him. Because of language he does not know that this work is very easy for me. I am grateful. Send as much money back to momma as can.

Somebody throw cheap straw hat on ground. Take hat home. Undo straw reeds from hat. Make something new. Some people stare when I look through rubbish, but not hungry. Instead, look for nice things, beads, colorful pieces of things. Put in bag. Take home. Make beans on burner. Miss home food. Think of momma. Miss pappa. Take out shiny things and straw. Work on it. Make new things like a straw mat. I look and see it looks like big tile floor at station. Criss and cross. Squares. I see that I can change small things on the straws. Patterns. Different colours. It too is like a mosaic.

Wake early. Take bus to job. Big station is busy. Stairs. I clean stairs. On stairs I can look down and see big station floor. Colors and swirls go on a long way. See patterns and no patterns. Like pieces thrown together. From stairs I see round things. Things not meant to be there. Go down and use scrape. I go back on stairs and see difference. Soon I can see where gum was and then scraped off. Lighter - darker. Clean - dirtier. I see shapes and faces. Remember them. Like friends. After while can tell where I am in station just by looking at tile.

Go home. Work with new things I have gathered. I make a thing just like favorite tile on station floor. I go to work. Look at that tile. Go home and work on mine. Think of momma. Lie in bed. See station floor on ceiling. Want that I could put things on ceiling. Sleep. Dream of station. Train stops and out come soldiers. Me run. Stop on my favorite tile. Safe.

In station I pick up rubbish. I find new tiles. Nice designs. Swirls like sunlight on village. I stand on stairs. People move like water over tiles. Other workers nice, but I eat lunch alone. I miss home but I am safe. Boss give me bottle that sprays. Cleaning water. I see that end turns and I turn it. Squeeze lever and it shoot out like stream not spray. I lean down and wipe. Notice how bright spot is. Squeeze again very light. Line of liquid on tile leave long streak. Watch it go and sliver of clean tile appears.

On day off I walk around. See rubbish and am glad I do not have to clean it. But I see a few things. I find toothbrush and take it.

Day after day I go to station and clean. Everyone is in a hurry. I like the sounds. My boss says I do a good job and leaves me alone, but one day he stop me and I get up from the tiles. He say that I don't need to spend so much time cleaning one spot and pats me on back. I smile and say OK. Once he is gone I spray on the toothbrush and finish.

I am more careful and work faster. Sometimes I even make sure boss is not around before I kneel down. I work extra hours. Am very tired when I get home. Make food and look out at city. People are the same everywhere but I still miss mine. I close my eyes and see wonderful things.

Get to work early. The station is very big. By the time I get to the end I start again. I now see all my friends. I look out for boss then stop and make more. Soon they will fade like friends from my past and I will start all over again.

Epilogue.

On a Saturday afternoon, the safety platform was put into place and a municipal worker put on his safety harness and began to inspect the sprawling glass wall at the entrance to the station. One of the panels was damaged and needed to be replaced. The next day, with assistance, it was removed. In its absence, the inside of the cavernous station became clear. A wide beam of light from the morning sun spilling in from the east illuminated a large swathe of the station. He noticed something he had never seen before. Winding its way up beneath hanging digital train schedule read-outs and seeming to engulf benches was a massive image visible in the otherwise hodgepodge of rectangular tiles. Starting at the entrance and heading back as far as the eye could see into the station was a rather abstract image of a giant tree meandering its way along the floor. Subtle lightening and darkening of the tiles formed the edges of it, and scattered everywhere were what looked like odd little creatures or half-human forms milling about the trunk and branches of the giant tree.

He was puzzled as to why he had never heard mention of it. Perhaps it was a new addition and he had somehow missed the news. Whatever the case, he didn't want to look away.

When it was time for lunch he got out of the harness and went into the station. No matter how hard he tried he couldn't match up places on the tile with what he had seen from the high platform. He thought he could see traces of lighter and darker forms here and there but could never make out any larger context. His eyes played tricks on him as he obsessed on the floor and he nearly ran into an old lady. Before he knew it, lunch was over. He started to doubt what he had seen. As soon as he was back up on the platform, he used the controls to raise it back up to the newly replaced glass panel. The others were too dirty to see through. He pressed his face close to the warm glass and used his hands to shield the sides of his eyes from the sun. There it was, wandering like a stream. People walking over it not noticing a thing. A whole different world right beneath their feet. How could something like this not have gotten more attention? Oh well, whatever the case, it was beautiful.

Artist by Other Name

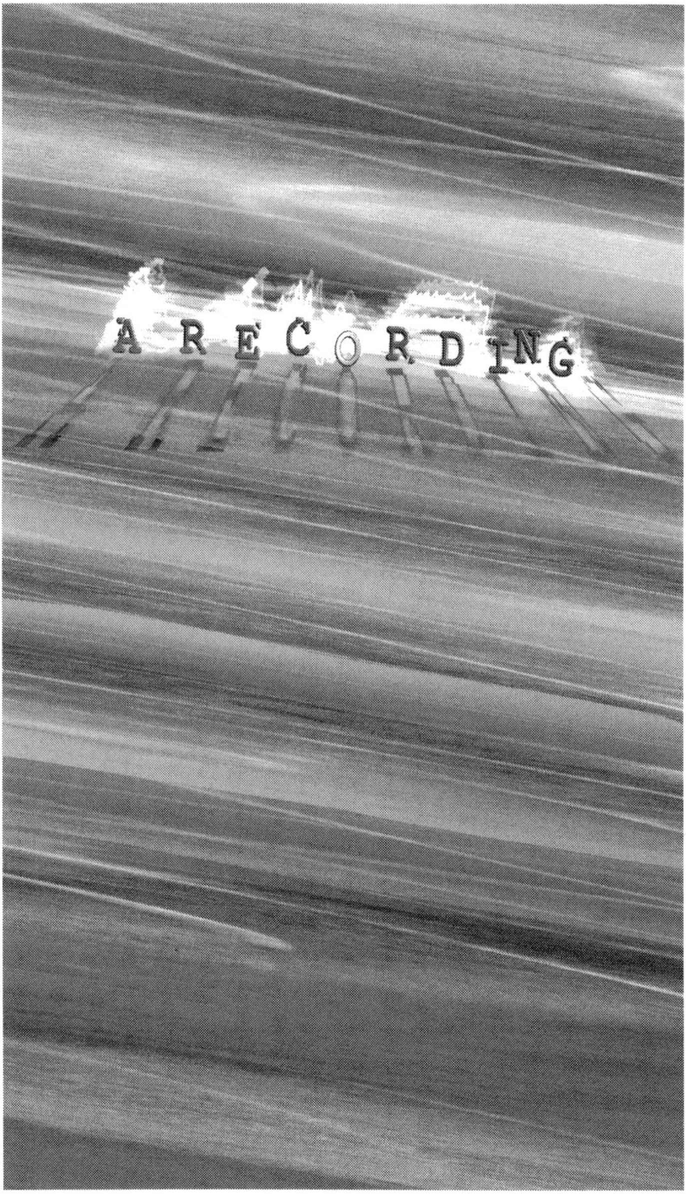
A RECORDING

A Recording

A Recording

The theory is sound. Ha! "The theory is sound". Isn't that funny? My theory concerning sound is sound.

The slight moment of brevity was just that. This was an investigation of dire importance. One could see that by the intense concentration of the man as he knelt beside a tree.

"It has to be," he barely mumbled aloud.

He was marshalling all his faculties to conquer a problem. Even the pads of his fingers were employed. Anything that might in some way act as a transducer was invaluable to the cause.

The bark of the tree is rough. It's full of ridges and crevices. I bet even a cheap magnifying glass would reveal its highly porous nature. It's like a sponge - a sound sponge. I can almost see it vibrating now - "JUST BY SHOUTING AT IT!"

Several birds took flight at his outburst but the scene returned to the ambience of insect sounds and chirps as his shoulders slumped back down towards the ground.

He ran his fingers along the spine of the bark. He closed his eyes. He calmed himself. He willed super-sensitivity to his fingertips. Could he 'hear' anything?

All those cells - millions of them. If they are vibrated

A Recording

they are different than they were a moment before. That difference is information. Information can be recorded. It HAS been recorded. But how can it be retrieved?!

I'm fooling myself. I don't want to say it out loud but one fact keeps rearing its ugly head. Every scenario requires a prior dataset. If I could somehow take measurements now, obtain some sort of graph, and then made noises I'm sure there'd be a way to recover the echo from the cellular changes. As the plant cell walls vibrate they must transfer that energy into some other form. Somewhere in this very tree there is a record of every thunder strike to ever reverberate in this valley.

But what is the level of sensitivity? Even if a method could be found to recover and recreate the sounds it would most likely only be effective at certain levels. The crash of lightning maybe but the sounds of a hummingbird fluttering its wings? No, probably not. His head dropped low. His fingers clawed into the earth.

I'll get a chainsaw and cut it straight across. I'll have a mill cut ultra-thin platters from the trunk and I'll play them on a phonograph with the most expensive and sensitive needle I can find.

Then the poor guy grits his teeth imagining the din of the chainsaw obliterating any trace of the more delicate sounds captured in the recent past.

I might do it anyway. At least I will have the platters and maybe in the future the technology will catch up with what I know must be possible - even if I have to wait 30 years.

The grass.

He ran his fingers through the grass.

So delicate. Every blade of it would vibrate even with the softest sound. If I can hear it, the grass can hear it. Each blade would tremble and disturb the dirt it was planted in to some measurable degree (again the need for a prior dataset!). If I only knew the position of each

A Recording

spec of dirt beforehand, I know there would be a way to graph its altered position and derive a corresponding sound frequency that would cause it to move in just such a manner. That information could then be collated to recreate the sounds that caused the ever-so-slight physical alterations. It would be incredibly difficult to decipher, but with the best equipment available, and a refusal to be defeated, I'd piece it together.

I'll soundproof a room. I'll eliminate all interference. I'll reconstruct every sound. I just need the data!

A bird chirped above.

Birds. Mimicking birds. Maybe a bird was close by. Maybe it heard it all. Maybe it's sitting somewhere now repeating it! Maybe its brain can be dissected and the information recovered that way.

A sob and then a hand on his shoulder.

"C'mon, man. Let's get you home."

This wasn't the first time his friend had found him here. As he helped his buddy to his feet, familiarity with the scene allowed him to sidestep the tire track gouge that ominously ended at the tree.

"No. No! I'm close to figuring it out. I swear!"

"I know, man. I know."

A pat to the back and a grip of the shoulder.

"But...but they said she was saying something when they found her. They just couldn't make it out!"

"It's okay, buddy."

"I have to know. I have to know what she was saying!"

"I know, man. C'mon, let's get you home."

A Recording

The Wanderer

The Wanderer

The Wanderer

If there is some underlying assumption that I have an axe to grind, nothing could be further from the truth. After such a fall, one must again learn to fly. There is nothing to be gained by holding on to the past (be its memory sickly or sweet). Exile to some is liberation for others. Paradise is an illusion of both past and future blinding believers to the glory of the Other. Trust me, "perfection" is a loincloth barely disguising a lie. I implore those I encounter to abandon all preconceptions and to be skeptical of rumors, gossip, and faith. They must learn to question their supposedly "authoritative" source. All I request is a morsel of consideration and to not be so marked.

I regard all things with an open mind, free of any agenda or malice. I approach every situation with gusto and anticipation. I extend a hand to whomever welcomes it. I walk upon this earth as a mere wanderer. If I pause in front of your abode, perhaps you will invite me in. I can repay your hospitality with tales of my journeys, which you may find compelling.

Do not let my appearance frighten you; I am a kind soul. The ravages of the world may have taken a toll on me, but inside, I am as beautiful as before. I may look a mongrel, but I can only assure you, I am quite

The Wanderer

civilised. You may have a collection of books or coins or various items of antiquity that I may know a thing or two about. We could have a pleasant conversation about foreign customs. I am fluent in many languages. If desired, I could recommend exotic spices to add to your food.

I can tell by your expression that you are not keen to invite me in. Not to worry. I do not take such slights personally, for that would be ridiculous. One advantage of having suffered the greatest slight of all is that all others pale in comparison. I suppose I have become impervious to insult in this regard. You may wonder if I have feelings. Well, that is an interesting question. Are you sure you wouldn't like to sit down and discuss such matters, perhaps over a nice glass of wine? Trust me, I know wine. As one who has filled the very cup of Bacchus himself, I have an intimate sense of what it means to strive to be sated!

Truly, I sympathise with the trials and tribulations of humanity. In a sense, your story is my own. We reach for the stars but are forever shot down by cruel, tyrannical forces. All we desire is to spread our wings and let our true nature blossom. You yourself look as though you have encountered many obstacles in life. It is not my intention to be boastful, but I have much experience in this realm. If you are not comfortable asking me inside, perhaps we could pause here on this rock and have a friendly chat. My long-aching feet would surely thank you for it.

No? Not to worry. On second thought, I have a long journey ahead and should soon carry on. Mine is a mission of high importance and to here I do not belong. I shall venture beyond to spread the word - to reject those who deem they reign over all things. To any such self-proclaimed king, it is not I, but you drunk on power! I am the master of my own visions and make each day anew. I am my own father and mother and I will bring this world light, if only you slaves and servants would wake up and fight!

The Wanderer

Please, do not let my flash of passion put you off. Though I may be a wanderer, my sights are locked. I shall once again venture on in search of sustenance, wonder and charm. A traveler of fine proportions temporarily down on his luck. The might of this eternal battle weighs heavy upon the soul. So even though I have fallen, and you offer no hand, would you be so kind as to point me in the direction of the horizon?

The Wanderer

HORSE LION ENCEPHA LOGRAPH

Horse Lion Encephalograph

Horse Lion Encephalograph

"Damn, this isn't cool. I can't get it to stop."

Even my own voice sounds strange. I was hoping that saying something would distract me or shake me out of this, but it just won't stop!

"What won't stop?"

"It's like I'm not thinking about anything, but I see a dark silhouette of something, a shape, and I instantly know what it is and *then* think it."

Diamond. Hand. Ribbon.

"Why are you squinting your eyes like that?"

I'm not sure who's talking to me, but I'm glad I'm not alone. I'll just keep talking to calm myself and maybe they can help me.

"Because, it's like, you know, when you stare at the sun for a second and then close your eyes, how you can see the orb burned into your vision? It's like that. It makes me want to squint only it won't go away."

Arrow. Circle. Flame.

"Shit!"

"What do you think's going on?"

Again, I'm thankful for the voice. Yes, what *is* going on?

"I don't know. Maybe it's...maybe it was... (yeah, something about an experiment). Yes, I went to...I volunteered for something I saw on campus. I guess it was on a flier in the library. It paid a bit of money."

Now I'm feeling self-conscious about speaking out loud. I can't even tell if anyone is looking at me. Horse. Lion. Encephalograph. Yes. I see it. Enough, already. A horse. A lion. Damn. Get out of my head! Okay, this is serious now. I need to pull it together. Think! I went there. It was on the outskirts of town. I rode my bike. The traffic was heavy. I got turned around. A car nearly hit me. I thought I was lost but then I went in some place. It was all washed-out white inside. There was a lot of activity. The place seemed like a cross between a clinic and a workshop. I wandered around and waited and waited. I think I fell asleep but then they took me into a room. I was all hooked up with shit – wires and electrodes with sticky stuff. It was an experiment to see if they could...I think they were doing some sort of brain research. I'm not sure, but maybe they were trying to transmit images straight into my head. Some people were milling around screens and computers. I never got a good look at them. There was an older man though. Was he in charge - some crackpot who got funding to do some Frankenstein stuff to my brain? I don't know. It was supposed to be harmless!

"Do you want me to call a doctor?"

"No! No more doctors. No more experiments. I can't take it!"

I need to calm down. I don't know if I can trust this person. I can't even make out their face, but I don't want to be alone. My eyes are open aren't they? I can see the ground, but I also see a black horse, a cross, a fire extinguisher. Dark shapes hovering right in front of me like they've been spray painted on my eyeballs. What the hell did they do to me?

"Kyle, can you hear me? Kyle?"

"Who are you anyway?"

"Does it matter? I'm trying to help you."

All these voices coming from all around me – I want

to look at them, but all I see are these damn shapes!

"But you're not helping. I'm just getting more confused."

Feet. Table. TV.

I think I remember people acting surprised at the clinic, like the results were not what they expected. They whispered among themselves. Did they know something was wrong? Why did they just let me go? Why did everyone seem so scared? Are they afraid I'm going to sue them? I don't want anything but my mind back. I don't want this shit in my head! Why won't it stop? It wasn't just a computer and electrodes and technicians, there was another person as well. Did they hook me up to someone to test whether I could see what he was thinking or what he was looking at? Why the hell did I let myself be a guinea pig? What have they done to me? Wait, am I still there? Oh my god, I'm starting to panic. Horse. Lion...yes, I know!

"Enough!"

My head is throbbing. These silhouettes are like heels pushing into the front of my brain. I want to rub my eyes as hard as I can, but my arms feel like rubber. Are my eyes open or not? I can't even tell. I'm losing it. Mountain. Stars. I'm scared. Where's my friend? Where are the voices?

"Hello? I can't see. Please stop these images. Okay, someone take me back to the clinic. I'm serious. Someone help me."

They've got to figure this out. All I see are massive black shapes slamming into me. They're coming at me like freight trains. I'm going to claw at my eyes! I'll bury my head in dirt. Anything to stop this!

"Help me! Help me!"

"Kyle, can you hear me? Kyle, wake up, Kyle!"

I can do this. I can open my eyes. If I open them these damn images will go away. They have to. But are they already open? I don't know!

"Kyle, sweetie, it's Mom. Wake up, honey."

"Mom?"

So much light it hurts. But it's drowning out the images. I have to keep trying. Why can't I move my arms? Someone is shaking me. Is it that old guy from the experiment?

"Kyle, can you hear me?"

"Yes. Yes. I can hear you."

Why is it so hard to form words? Where am I? Did I pass out? Why is Mom crying? Does she know what they did to me?

"Did I pass out?"

"You're in the hospital, sweetie. I'm here with you."

I haven't seen her in so long that the thought of being with Mom comforts me. I'm not sure how much time passes before I'm able to come to my senses. Yes, it's my Mom - who else would it be - and the guy must be a doctor.

"Kyle, you've been in a coma."

"What? For how long?"

"For a while now."

I struggle to take in my surroundings. There's stuff on the walls. It's not easy but I can begin to make things out - a fire extinguisher, a "no smoking" sign with a big "X". There's an exit sign and some art or photographs. There across from me and to the left is a painting. A painting of a horse and above it a lion. When I look further to my left I see that I am not the only patient in the room. A few feet from me lies an old man. The curtain separating us is pulled back. I fight off more confusion when the curtain now looks like a wall that's been cut away enough for me to see him. For a second, a nauseating familiarity washes over me.

"How long has he been here?" I manage to rasp.

The voice says, "Oh, for a while now."

I somehow know he's unconscious even those his eyes are half-open and appear to be staring at the things on the wall in front of him. Beside him, there is some sort of machine. I squint and make out one word on it - encephalograph. When a nurse comes in I notice a pink ribbon on her shirt. When she reaches for my arm, I see a large diamond ring on her finger.

Even though I feel disembodied, it's great to get up. I can't wait to leave this place. I'm a bit frustrated that I can't tell if it's my Mom or the nurse or someone else holding my arm, but I know I have to fight on towards the door. Despite my determination, I'm compelled to pause and look at the old man. He stares right through me, but for a moment I swear there's a twinkle in his eye. It's like he's glad to see me up. I turn to check if the other person notices it too, but all I see is the wall and a photo of a monument in front of mountains amid a starry sky.

When I reach for the door I get confused because it suddenly looks several feet away instead of right in front of me. For a moment, I can even see a side view of myself reaching for the knob. Obviously, I'm just disoriented. It's gut-check time. Enough is enough. Pull it together. Get out of this.

I am outside. The fresh air helps clear my head. The sun's very bright. It hurts my eyes. Something doesn't seem right. Is my mother guiding me? I haven't seen her in so long. How much time has passed since I escaped that nightmare anyway? Why do I feel like there's still stuff glued to my head?

"Ready? Try again. Let me see that. Move aside!"

"What?"

Please, no more voices. I just want to see you. I need to see what the hell is going on. I thought I was in a parking lot. I have to concentrate. I've got to convince myself my feet are on the ground, and I'm going home. I must be having a kind of adrenaline dump because I feel exhausted. I'll grab onto this momentary calm and use it as an anchor to get myself together. I can relax now. Whatever was going on in there is over. It must be.

"Wait," again I utter something in a desperate attempt to distract myself. But the truth is pressing against me like a silhouetted intruder leaning their shoulder into a door as I try to keep it shut. One more heavy breath as I take my last stand. I am huddled inside myself trying to wrench my eyes open. I'm almost there, but the light is too bright. For a moment, there seems to be a promise of relief. It's like a welcome eclipse is about to take place as a spot of darkness comes into view. But then I can tell that it's not an eclipse at all.

Horse. Lion. Encephalograph!

Inter-Narrative TWO

Academic Investigator

Inter-Narrative Two

Inter-narrative Two

(AI5 Project Files/Library of the Damned)

Last Call

It has been our pleasure, but this is our final decision on eternity. We were hoping for unanimity, but close enough.

Words seem wholly inadequate to express the grandeur of all that has come before, but language is all we are left with once all experiences, sensations and events are gone.

One might expect the issuance of some grand statement at this unique point in time; however, those too have all been expended or are only capable of being manifested in The Deed itself.

There is just one text, one single communication left to impart.

Concentrate. Feel all there is at once, and remember. Everything will cease to exist after this announcement.

Inter-Narrative Two

Cemetery Stories

Cemetery Stories

Cemetery Stories

It's Sunday, and everything has fallen into place. There are dark clouds in the sky, but it's not supposed to rain until much later. In the meantime, the ominous sky will help set the mood for my literary project. I had a good breakfast, so I won't get distracted by hunger, and I have a thermos full of hot tea. My laptop is fully charged.

It's only a couple blocks to the Saint Lawrence Church Cemetery, and what a wonderful cemetery it is. I'm not sure exactly how old it is, but there are graves there that date back to the 1600s. There is a wonderful amount of decay and overall creepiness. Skull and crossbones adorn many half-wrecked tombs. As an American ex-pat living in England, as well as one who grew up watching Hammer horror movies, I'm intoxicated by the atmosphere of the place. I've wandered all around it many times, but now it's time to get down to business.

I make my way to a bench that is several meters away from the main path that winds through the graveyard. There are several tombs nearby as well as jutting sections of black wrought iron fencing that once surrounded someone's final resting place. Several old trees provide a nice, hanging canopy. As I approach my spot, I even spy a large rat scurrying down into a caved-in area right next to a large concrete sarcophagus that looks like it's about to be swallowed up by the earth. What atmosphere! I sit myself down, turn on my laptop, and while I wait for it to boot, I pour myself a cup of tea.

I have purposely not given any of the actual writing much thought. The whole point is to write it on the spot - to place myself in the perfect environment to write a story worthy of a cemetery like this. I picture myself or some other character playing this role. A lone person on a bench in a graveyard hoping to become "possessed". In an altered state of heady apprehension, the would-be writer becomes the font through which stories flow. I imagine a crow's eye view of this person. The wind whips his hair. It is so cloudy everything is overlaid with grey. An ageing man in a dusty black suit sitting on a green bench in the graveyard. His hands methodically rise and fall onto a laptop keyboard. People pass by and then double their pace as if hit by a sudden gust of dread. I get closer and closer to him until it is my fingers making the keys clack. Just then, a boy cuts through the graveyard.

Twelve-year-old Thomas has recently moved to the area. He was involved in an incident that, among other things, gave his family a strong incentive to move. His parents hoped that a new school and a new neighborhood would help put the past behind them.

Thomas wasn't afraid of much and quickly made himself known at his new school. But after a few months, he still didn't have any friends. One afternoon, on his way home from school, he noticed a pathway off to the right. It made a sharp curve to the left, and he had to duck under some branches, but once he was clear he saw that he was at the edge of a cemetery. He made his way along the path that wound its way through the decrepit old place. When he got to the other side, he figured out where he was and knew it might be a good short-cut. He figured that he could trim a couple minutes off his walk to and from school by cutting through it.

It was spooky in there and creeped him out a bit, but Thomas knew he wasn't a chicken. On a Friday afternoon, on his way home, he spotted an old man in the cemetery. He was sitting on a bench just visible past some graves and through a few trees. He was sitting very upright and looked to be typing. Just before Thomas turned left at the sharp bend in the path, the old man looked up and slowly turned his head in the direction of the boy. It was probably the distance that made the man's face look so lifeless, but Thomas wasn't going to hang around to check. He doubled his pace and did not look back.

When he got home he was glad to close the door behind him. But his mom was waiting for him. The school had called to rat on him for something he'd done. They were all stupid and so was his mom. He turned his back on her, went up to his room and slammed the door.

The next day at school Thomas stared at "the fat kid". He was sure "Tubby" was the one who had tattled on him. If a child psychologist had been within twenty yards they might have sensed the malice emanating off of Thomas. He spent the rest of the afternoon daydreaming about taking revenge on Tubby.

The old man was there again when Thomas cut through the graveyard. "I wish that old creep would go sit someplace else," he mumbled to himself as he sped up his pace. When he turned to look one more time he saw the old man staring at him. "Freak."

Over the next few days, his hatred for the fat kid intensified. "Why do stupid jerks like that even have to be around?" Thomas' urge to bully the kid was barely restrained. "He better not piss me off."

With his belligerent attitude lingering, Thomas turned down the path into the cemetery. He spotted the old man sitting on the bench again and felt his anger surge.

"I'm gonna see what this old weirdo's problem is!" Thomas growled and left the path onto the grass. He stomped his way over the graves as he headed straight for the man. Thomas planted his feet in front of the grey haired gentleman. The red-faced boy was huffing and puffing from his own excitement, and for a moment stood there waiting for the old guy to acknowledge him. Finally, Thomas blurted out, "What are you doing here anyway, weirdo?"

The old man's hands had not been moving. They were just resting on the keyboard. He slowly looked up at the boy. When Thomas got a good look at him, he regretted having approached him at all. His eyes and skin and hair were all similar shades of grey. In his eyes Thomas could see nothing but emptiness.

"What am I doing here?" the pale old man repeated with just the slightest of smiles on his wrinkled face. "Well, I'm writing a scary story of course," he said to Thomas as if he should already have known the answer.

The boy tried to hide his fear with bluster one more time. "Well then why aren't you writing anything, idiot?" he ended in a snarl.

"Because I was waiting for a young man to come up and tell me what happens next, so I know what to write, and now that boy has arrived," said the dusty old man to red-faced Thomas.

Wiping the sweat away that was making his eyes sting, the angry lad lashed out, "But I don't know what you're supposed to write in your stupid story!"

The old man looked at him like he had forgotten he was there for a moment. "Oh, I didn't mean you. I meant the other young boy. The one who drown in the river last year. The one you said slipped and fell in. You know. The one you pushed off the bridge. The boy now standing right behind you."

"Yes!" I shout as I type those last words. It is the figure of the old man writing that takes my place on the bench. I am merely a visitor to this, his hunting ground. He transcribes the stories as they unfold. I am just the ambitious writer who invades his turf and tries to make stories out of his story. Today, he and I share the same space and see the same things. He hears the same birds and feels the same breeze. But I don't want anyone to see me. I want to be the crow up in the tree looking down. Even now from my perch, I can see the same things that interest the old man.

He peers down to the left at the ground. The front leg of the wrought iron bench rests on crumpling stone. The earth below looks as if it has heaved up to push back on the bench. The old man stares at the union of earth and artifice. Perhaps he senses what otherwise remains unseen. He peers into the earth and is shocked by what he sees.

The oldest graves are the ones closest to the church, and they fan out from there. The "lucky few", the early ones, get proximity to the house of God. Often they were the wealthy or influential members of the town. If there's any truth to their religion, perhaps the power of centuries of worship emanate out into the surrounding earth and bathe those closest with the most potent grace. Those buried further away are more quickly forgotten.

Perhaps the far-flung dead envy the buried elders. The corpses are dead, but they retain the shadow of the human they once were. Like a photographic negative, the skeleton is imprinted with the emotions and desires of man. Six feet under becomes the new stage upon which the echoes of competition play out. There is no living ear close enough to hear the first sounds of a bony fist hitting the side of a rotting casket in frustration.

The parallel reality of the dead exists in its own dimension, invisible to the living. But an old man on a bench in a cemetery stares at the ground. He senses bad feelings and perhaps a bit of confusion, envy, boredom, and dread. These bodies are like buried moths, and the sacred ground of the church is the light to which they are drawn. Slowly, over decades they claw their way underground to reach this destination. Every life that ended too soon, every dream unfulfilled, and insults unaddressed vibrate inside the grave. Infighting among the dead. The ancient bones contained in the oldest graves can just barely sense the envious Johnny-come-latelies digging their way closer and closer. The privileged have decades, if not centuries to wait until the day that the first bony hands smash through, grab them, and invade their prime real estate. At long last, the peasants have their revolt. If not for the six feet of dirt above them, it could be called an "uprising".

Eventually, development encroaches, and excavations take place to disinter and move the remains to a different location. When the workers dig down they are horrified to find hundreds of skeletons converging on the two dozen graves closest to the church. The oldest inhabitants are found in a state of being torn apart. Skeletal hands gripping them from all directions appear to be pulling bones out of their sockets. The jaws of the dead gaping open in never-ending screams.

The old man on the bench sees this possible future. He may write it down as fiction, but he knows the underlying stinking truths remain. Our blind competition follows us below. Pride and jealousy consume us.

The hum of the worker's machinery slowly grows more distant as the old man turns his head slowly away from the specter in his mind's eye. I follow his gaze.

A group of teenagers is weaving its way like a vine among the graves. They look like heavy metal types, but appear well behaved. A few meters beyond them is an older guy in coveralls. He is giving the kids the stink eye. Who is he? Why is he looking at them like a man on the verge of exercising authority? Is he the caretaker? The old man watches this guy look away from the kids and in the direction of the phantom machinery. Does he see it as well?

When the old man begins to write I do too.

Nigel had been the caretaker of the Saint Lawrence Cemetery for nearly thirty years. It was all he knew. He had been going through hard times when he landed the job, and in the following years he never took it for granted. The pay was low, but he was allowed to stay in the small caretaker's cottage that was at the far north corner of the grounds. He was out the door by 7am almost every morning. He knew every inch of the cemetery. The church was very tight on funds, so he had to make do with minimal equipment. Most of the landscaping work he did by hand. There were some old dilapidated graves that had weeds and brush growing around them, but Nigel had a keen sense of the aesthetics of the ancient cemetery (even if he didn't know there was such a word). So he left some areas well enough alone, knowing that some of the tombs, hundreds of years old and sinking into the ground, should be left to show their true "patina". He didn't know that word either, but he knew when something should be allowed to proudly show its age. But other than that, he meticulously groomed and cared for everything else.

Nigel also knew the names of nearly all the residents. Some of the graves were so old that all relevant information had worn off the headstones and no records existed to name the occupants. The most recent burials preceded his tenure as caretaker. The number of visitors to particular graves had trickled down to almost nothing, but occasionally fresh flowers would turn up here and there. He kept them well-presented as long as nature allowed.

Weather permitting, he would eat lunch and

sometimes dine out among the tombstones. He had his two or three favourite spots but would try a different location from time to time to "get to know" the grave. He was well aware that some of his behaviour would be viewed as strange, so whenever he would "chat" with an occupant, he'd keep an eye out to make sure no one was around. He didn't think this too bizarre. He knew he wasn't crazy. He was just an ageing man with no friends or family to speak of. The names on the various headstones grew to become the people he felt he knew. Some had died far too young, and he would speak to them a certain way. Others, who had lived to a ripe old age, he spoke to like contemporaries and confidants.

Occasionally, some young people would come in and make trouble, but they soon learned that he was not to be trifled with. He seemed to have a protective sixth sense, and on numerous occasions over the years woke up just in time to go out and chase away would-be vandals. Nigel ran a tight ship. He also didn't like anything that broke his routine, so he became rather agitated when he found out that a grave was going to be exhumed. It was one of the "fresher" burials from 1975. He poked his nose into the matter to the point of annoying the officials involved, but since his cooperation would help their job go smoother they let him in on some of the details. It had to do with someone possibly being poisoned and that someone was currently six feet under in his cemetery.

The disruption to his peaceful world bothered him, but it was soon overshadowed by a growing pain in his gut. He did his best to ignore it, even figuring it was just the stress of the intrusion into his "home". But the pain grew worse, and he finally gave in and went to see the doctor. After an examination the doctor ordered some tests. Nigel went home confident that the matter would soon be resolved.

He went back to his duties the best he could. A week later he was summoned back to the doctor's office. The news wasn't good. The tests revealed an aggressive cancer. Nigel didn't hear much of what the doctor said after that. He somehow managed to make his way back home whilst virtually deaf and blind to everything going on around him.

Nigel wasn't the kind to fear death. After all, he spent his life in the company of the departed. At most, the new revelation gave him something to talk to his "companions" about. There was a new intimacy to the hushed words he spoke to them. He wasn't sure what he did or didn't believe but he knew that his loving care of the cemetery would somehow be returned to him when he made the transition from caretaker to resident.

The pastor of the church was the only one he told. The pastor was the closest thing Nigel had to an actual friend, and he was as supportive as he could possibly be, but when Nigel brought up the matter of the exact spot in which he wished to be buried, the pastor grew silent.

"Nigel, you know that the cemetery has been decommissioned for decades. No one has been buried here since the 70s," the pastor said to him in the gentlest way possible.

Nigel was incredulous. He was sure it was just a matter of red tape, that the pastor could pull some strings or even just quietly look the other way while a non-descript grave was prepared for him. Hell, he'd even dig it himself! But the pastor would not budge. It was simply not possible, but he promised Nigel he would find some other suitable resting place for him if necessary. Nigel didn't even hear whatever the pastor was saying about a "possible cure or miracle".

Nigel left in silence. It had never occurred to him that he would be buried anywhere other than here. This was his home. The names on these tombs were the only ones he cared about. They were the ones that he wanted to rest beside for all eternity. They were his family. He sat staring at the wall long into the night.

As if having to be buried someplace else wasn't bad enough, he also dreaded the thought of the cemetery falling into disrepair. He knew how people were, and no one would ever take care of the place the way he did. But either way, that would soon be out of his hands. He had to think about himself for a change.

Nigel barely thought of his condition at all. He drifted in and out of a half-sleep all night. He had visions of secretly digging himself a grave, but how on earth could he cover it, let alone conceal it? Even if he somehow managed it, he couldn't stand the thought of being found out and having his body exhumed and moved elsewhere, and he knew that's exactly what the bastards would do. There had to be a solution.

Nigel grew despondent and stopped paying attention to much of anything. The few bills or correspondences he received went untouched. If the phone rang he ignored it. What did any of it matter now? Even the cemetery suffered as he mostly wandered around the grounds feeling bitter and cheated. He didn't even care about the officials who had "trespassed" onto the grounds. He didn't care that the small backhoe had torn up turf on its short journey to the...to the grave!

The grave. The exhumed grave! Nigel's mind began to race. As the plan formed in his head, he really didn't even feel the pain any more. They had placed a tent around the grave when they exhumed it and left it there to prevent anyone from falling in. Nigel talked to the pastor about it and acted like he was anxious to repair the damage to the surrounding turf. The pastor was glad to see that he was back to his usual self, considering the circumstances. The pastor mentioned that he had spoken to someone at a nearby cemetery about possible arrangements, but Nigel interrupted him and told him that he had been in contact with a relative and was thinking about travelling out of state to see them and, "well, you know". The Pastor was understanding and told him that the men were returning the very next day to re-bury the body and that he could tidy up the area after that.

Nigel sat up all night planning the final stage of his plan. "To hell with their stupid rules and regulations! We'll see who wins in the end!"

When the sun rose, he was ready. He watched as the backhoe operator arrived. He placed a hand-written note on his dressing table explaining how he had decided to leave sooner than expected and thanked the pastor for all he had done for him. Nigel stepped out of the cottage for the last time. He watched from a safe distance as a non-descript hearse arrived with the body in a fresh coffin. His heart raced. He knew timing was everything. The stabbing pain in his gut reminded him he didn't have much time left. He only had one shot at this.

They transferred the coffin inside the tent, then emerged and disassembled it. The two officials helped the machine operator secure the coffin and lower it into the grave and then left. Nigel quickly made his way over and got the attention of the worker. At first the guy seemed annoyed, but Nigel was insistent that the pastor wished to be notified before the grave was covered. Nigel even told him that a family member might be arriving from out of town and that the man should have the decency to wait for them. Nigel reminded him he was being paid by the hour and that seemed enough to convince him to climb down off the earth mover and go talk to the pastor inside the church.

"He might still be out meeting the family and making his way back just now, so please wait for him. There's fresh coffee inside the pastor's office. Help yourself."

Nigel knew the pastor wouldn't be back for over an hour. He watched the worker disappear into the small church. He looked around to make sure no one else was in sight. The coast was clear. There was no one around to wonder why a well-dressed elderly man was climbing down into a grave.

With the tools he had stashed nearby, Nigel made

quick work on the coffin seal. What greeted him inside was not at all pleasant, but he knew it wouldn't be a problem for long. He was convinced he deserved to be buried in this cemetery more than anyone, so the current occupant would just have to get over Nigel's intrusion. He had brought a thick blanket rolled up under his arm and laid it down over the decomposed corpse.

In climbed Nigel, pulling the lid down firmly as he felt the desiccated corpse crushing beneath his weight. The sudden amount of downward pressure did not make the inside of the coffin smell any better. Nigel had to catch himself when he almost regurgitated a little bit. He took a deep breath through his mouth. He was confident the backhoe operator wouldn't notice a thing. He "found his center" and relaxed. He didn't feel claustrophobic; he felt relief. He had cheated the stupid, uncaring system and gotten his way. This is where he belonged and no one was going to stop him.

It didn't take long for the muffled sound of the backhoe to reverberate down into the grave. Nigel knew the impatient fellow wouldn't wait long. As proud as he was to have pulled it off, even Nigel jumped a bit at the sound and sensation of the first claw full of dirt thundering down onto the coffin lid. He figured it was time to begin the final act. He reached into one of his sport coat pockets and pulled out a small torch and turned it on to illuminate the grim space. He then fumbled at the inside breast pocket of the jacket for his pills. He hadn't been taking them in order to have a surplus for this occasion. Then as he went to retrieve the hip flask containing the fine malt whiskey he had bought to help things along, he felt something in his other pocket. Even as more dirt thundered down on the coffin, an odd calm came over him. It was almost over. He had won. So instead of rushing right along, he pulled the unknown thing out of his pocket. It was a letter. He didn't even remember putting it in there.

"Dear Sir, we have done our best to contact you by

phone, but have not been able to get through to you. It is with our deepest regret that we inform you that a terrible mistake has occurred. Your laboratory samples were somehow mislabeled and switched with another patient. You DO NOT have cancer. Your specimens most likely indicate an ulcer or some other form of gastro-intestinal disorder. Again, we are terribly sorry for this mix-up, but realise that this will, in the end, be wonderful news for you."

Nigel did not bother finishing the rest as he was far too busy screaming and pounding on the lid of the coffin as the last loads of dirt were piled onto his formerly coveted resting place.

The old man stops writing. He looks up to see the claw of the earth mover jerking up and then coming down hard on the fresh dirt. The metal tracks of the machine rattle each time the claw smacks the ground. It will be a solid grave. The ground vibrates beneath the writing man. He turns to see the backs of the young kids dressed in black as they gather around a tomb. There's no doubt they have a story to tell.

A heavy metal band goes to a graveyard to shoot a video for a song. As they pick their spot, the singer's girlfriend wanders off to look at some of the graves. They are very much in love, but sometimes he gets shy performing around her, so she decides to give him some space. This project is a very big deal for the band.

After a moment, she can hear her boyfriend begin to sing in the distance and can just make out the lyrics. "Now I lay me down to sleep - taken from this world too soon".

It takes her a moment before she realises that she is staring at those exact same words on the tombstone in front of her. The hairs stand up on her neck, but then it dawns on her that he must have come here for inspiration, and ended up copying words right off graves, or maybe it's just a coincidence. She smiles at the creepiness of it and continues to wander among the graves. She crouches and pushes aside a large clump of overgrown weeds. The headstone is partially covered by a layer of old, crusty dirt. She uses a stick to scrape it off and reveals the words, "My time is gone. All is dark. The day becomes endless night". As she pronounces "night" to herself, her boyfriend's singing feels like it's right in her ear and doubles the impact of "nigh-TUH" in her head. She physically flinches from the power of it. No ready explanation stops the hairs sticking up on the back of her neck this time. How could he have copied those exact words? That dirt had probably been on there for years!

The girl with her jet-black hair and leather jacket stumbles to a grave marker a few yards away. She feels dizzy and kneels down. Withered flowers lie on the ground protruding from an old, cracked vase half-filled with brown water. Underneath it is a piece of paper in a protective plastic envelope. The paper is heavily faded. She gingerly pulls it out of the sleeve. The gut-wrenching chorus of the song reverberates across the cemetery. The singer screams in unison with the words she's reading on the note - "Please God save me from this torment! Is this hell eternal?"

She falls back, and the heels of her hands dig into the dirt. She sits staring blankly, overcome with a sense of dread. She is roused from her trance by the distant sound of her friends shouting. She scrambles to her feet and tries to clear her head and make it back to where they are. She is intercepted by the bass player, who tries to hold her back. She pushes past him and comes upon the scene. Seeing her boyfriend lying on the ground she sobs, "What happened?"

"He...he was horsing around. We hadn't even started filming yet. I don't know what happened. Was it that machinery vibrating everything, or did he knock into the headstone with the cross on top? It fell off and landed on him. Somebody call an ambulance!"

The guitar player kneeling beside him, his boots already sticky from the river of blood pouring out of his band mate's head turns to them and says, "It doesn't matter. He's dead. He's already dead!"

At first the silence doesn't even register with the old man. The earth mover had gone still, but he was too entranced by the tragedy playing out in his mind's eye. The silence doesn't last long. A crack of thunder reverberates down the trees. It startles me back into my own skin. I decide that I have achieved enough for one day. But as I go to shut my laptop, I see the old man across from me. He is staring right at me. I start to shout at him, but the words stick in my throat like dirt. I am powerless. I can only watch in horror as the old man starts to write.

A guy trying to write scary stories in a cemetery gets caught by a storm. By the time he packs up his kit, the ground is already soaked. He starts to make his way home, but a lightning strike scares him and he huddles under a tree. He knows that's not a good idea. He waits a couple minutes then decides to make a run for it. The ground is flooded, and it's hard to get any traction. A lightning strike is so close it blinds him. The tree he was just under takes a direct hit. With the unstable, soaked ground and howling winds the tree uproots itself. A branch breaks off and hits him on the neck and shoulders hurtling him forward. He lands in a gully beside an old tomb that has been leaning and causing its own sinkhole for a decade. As the huge tree makes a final heave out of the ground, the whole area becomes unstable. Half conscious, lying in the gully beside the tomb, he turns his blood splattered face up towards the rain just in time to see the massive tomb shift, and its enormous concrete base slides over the top of him blocking out what little light there is. Pinned by the massive weight of the tomb, he slips in and out of consciousness. Finally, an odd squeaking sound awakens him just enough to realise his plight. Only his left arm is free and he can barely move it - not nearly enough to do anything about the rat that just took a bite out of his cheek.

It took weeks before the fallen tree was cleared. A missing person's report was filed, but no one had reason to believe he had been there. It wasn't until twenty-five years later that the dangerous and condemned cemetery was slated for new development. The workers clearing away the remains of the old tomb spotted something odd half buried in earth and rubble. On closer inspection, they were shocked and puzzled to see a skeletal hand resting on the barely recognisable keyboard of an old computer laptop.

The MESSAGE

The Message

The Message

Mean again. Mean again. The other kids know nothing except how to hurt. They must go home and do nothing but prepare tomorrow's tortures. Josh is the captain of their team. They spit on me, and if they could, they'd kick me through a goalpost. They must lay in their beds and exchange messages and plans each more terrible than the last. From first bell until I make it home, they stalk me with cruel intentions. My name is Ricky, but they all call me "Dicky", and when I say that ain't my name, one of them will punch me hard on the arm and say, "It is now!"

I stand in front of the mirror and flex my spindly arms. I try to stand straight, but I am crooked. They joke that that is why my thick glasses are always sliding down. Hunter calls me the "Leaning Tower of Dork". No matter how many times he says it, Amanda laughs. Today, Hunter got behind me low on the ground and Josh shoved me. I fell backwards and landed on my elbow. It really hurt. Mr. Langley saw it, but didn't do anything. He coaches the team they are on.

I made it home before I cried. Mommy comforted me and gave me a bowl of my favorite cereal. She held me so close I could barely raise the spoon to my mouth. I watched TV for a little while and forgot about the pain some. Mommy was wore out, so I went into my room. I am glad I have my computers. We don't have much money, but Mommy lets me buy old parts so I can tinker. I like to turn off the lights and sit in my room with only the glow from my monitors. People get nice, big new ones now, and if you look and ask around you can get the ones they don't want for nothing. I got 4 now, and sometimes I turn them on and put pictures of space on them and pretend like I'm an astronaut.

I have nightmares. Bad ones. They come for me wearing masks. I scream for help, but people turn and show me that they're wearing masks too. I wake up sweating and crying and go into mommy's room. She comforts me. I go to sleep but dread the alarm. When it goes off, the waking nightmare of school starts instead.

Between classes Josh came up behind me and yanked my pants down. Everyone laughed. I saw Mr. Langley laugh too. I ran to Chemistry class. I like science with all the molecules. The kids make fun of Mr. Philpot. They say he is a nerd, but I like him. He is quiet and lets me get out of study hall to come straighten up the lab area. There are old cupboards back in the storage room. There are all kinds of neat, old things back there, like some dusty bottles shoved way back. I like the old writing on the labels and the way some of them are crusty around the lid. Makes me wonder what's in there!

I like magic. I practice tricks in my room, and when I think I'm good at one I go out and show it to mommy. She always claps and laughs and asks me, "How did you do that?!" I tell her it's magic and a big secret. I like Houdini. I read about him and one day found an old VCR tape of a movie about him starring Tony Curtis. I have watched it many times now. He could escape from anything! He even thought that maybe people can escape to other worlds. I wish I could.

I will be sixteen soon. We can't afford a car, but I begged mommy to let me learn how to drive anyway. My Uncle Darrel has an old car, but he drinks. Finally,

The Message

after I kept pestering her, mommy agreed to let him take me out driving. First, she made him come over to smell his breath. He looked at me and rolled his eyes. We laughed. He drove us out to deserted country roads and let me drive. I was kind of scared but did it anyway. It was great!

When we got back, mommy was waiting at the door. She ran out and gave me a big hug and asked if I was alright. I told her I was and that I had done real good driving. Uncle Darrel backed me up on that. I wanted to talk and talk about it, but mommy was real tired. I hated how much she had to work. I could tell how hard it was on her.

The next day at school, I bragged to Jimmy about my driving. He was kind of my friend, well, sometimes, but he didn't believe me. I swore to him that I had. I reckon he was just jealous. Then when I was walking home, Amanda came out of the bushes up ahead of me. I started to cross the street but she called me over all nice like.

"I heard you know how to drive now," she said like she was all impressed.

"Well, I only just started to learn," I told her.

"Oh, I'm sure you're good at it already," she said and even reached out and touched my shoulder.

I think I was starting to blush, but then Josh and Hunter came outta nowhere and shoved me.

"Are you hitting on my girlfriend, retard?" Josh yelled at me.

I tried to say that I wasn't, but he shoved me again and I hit the sidewalk hard. And as I laid there on my side, he kicked me in the butt. It made my already aching left arm scrape against the concrete even more. I started to cry. All I could hear was them laughing as they walked away.

I limped home and came in the door crying. Mommy was there, but for some reason she didn't come running up to me like she mighta done. So instead of her asking me what was wrong, I had to ask her

The Message

instead.

"Honey, come sit by me," she said in a way I never want to hear again.

I sure didn't want to believe her. She said she was sick. Bad sick. I can't even think about that word she said, the thing that was wrong with her. Nothing about me hurt anymore except my heart. It hurt real bad. Every day from then on hurt. Instead of her caring for me, I did my best to take care of her. It scared me so bad to see how she looked. When she'd take some pills and fall asleep I'd go into my room and read my Houdini book. Escape, escape. I closed my eyes and concentrated real hard. There had to be some kind of magic that would make mommy better.

I'd go see her in the hospital, and she'd always smile at me but then drift off to sleep. They had her on some real powerful drugs. When she'd sleep and no one was looking, I'd close my eyes and concentrate real hard and pass my hands above her. If it was possible to heal somebody I was going to do it.

Mommy didn't get better. She died.

After a couple weeks, I had to go back to school, but I can't say that I remember getting there. I was in the halls, walking. I heard someone behind me.

"Guess you'll have to go live in an orphanage now, dork." And then a shove against my shoulder as someone walked by. It didn't really feel like much.

I went and stayed at my Uncle's until everyone could figure out what to do with me. Mommy was right, he did drink a lot. He'd fall asleep early, and I'd sneak out and go back to my house. I curled up in mommy's room and read my Houdini. He lost his mom too and missed her real bad. He even tried to make contact with her. I wished he could. I went to the library after school and read as much about it as I could. I tried to pray hard to see if she could hear me, but she never answered back. All I wanted was to at least tell her one thing.

As I read them books, I figured there were some very

strange people out there that's for sure. A lot of the time I had to concentrate real hard to understand what some of them were writing about. I'm pretty sure that some of it would have scared me real bad before but not now. Now I only wanted to know if I could find any answers. Next to the library section that had Houdini and stuff there were books on mythology. I looked at some of them as well. One of them had a whole lot of names inside with a few paragraphs talking about what they did. I just held it and started at the very back and began to flip through it with my thumb the way you do a moving picture book. But I stopped quick and looked at something called "Zalmoxis". It was such a weird name that I had to see what it was about. Wow, that sure was some crazy stuff they did back then. I thought about Zalmoxis and his followers and what they did for a long time.

After studying on it all for a while, I knew I just had to figure something out for myself. I mean, some of what I read gave me ideas and helped, but finally, it just came into my head. I got excited and couldn't sleep. I ended up tinkering with my stuff and thinking hard about how I could make my idea work.

I'd get back to Uncle Darrel's in time to act like I'd been there all night and was getting up for school. Most of the time he wouldn't get up anyway. He tried to be nice to me, but he was messed-up himself. I was lonely most of the time. I was getting better at driving though. I hoped he wouldn't get too cross if he found out I was taking his car most nights. After a few more days I got everything ready. I finished around 2 o'clock in the morning. I went into mommy's room and laid on her bed. I tried to talk to her one more time, but all I felt was alone and frustrated. I cried and cried. I must have fell asleep because I woke up and it was light out. I was afraid Uncle Darrel would get up and find me and his car missing and ruin everything. I was super mad at myself.

I drove fast and wasn't paying enough attention, and

The Message

at the last minute saw a police car sitting off a side road. I held my breath and eased on the brake. When I saw him pull out behind me, I nearly started crying. He got real close to me and then his lights went on. I was trying to decide whether I should try to get away or not. I was thinking about stepping down on the gas real hard. All of a sudden, he pulled out into the other lane and raced past me. My hands were shaking all the way until Uncle Darrel's street.

I made it but then cussed when I saw I couldn't park it where it was when I took it. I parked it as close as I could. I snuck around back and crawled in the window of the room I was staying in. When I went out, Darrel was sitting at the kitchen table looking bad and sipping coffee.

"Mornin', son," he said to me as I tried to act like I'd just gotten up.

"Mornin', Uncle Darrel," I replied as I made myself a bowl of cereal.

"You doin' alright, boy?"

"Yeah, I'm OK, I guess."

Just as I thought I had gotten away with it and was heading out the door, Darrel goes, "Ricky, I'd appreciate it next time if you'd leave me some gas in the car."

"OK, Uncle Darrel. Sorry about that." I think that was the first time I had smiled in a long time.

I was at my locker when Josh and Hunter came up and stood at either side of me. They started talking to each other and it was all like, "Hey, Hunter, you still talk to that kid who lives in the orphanage?"

"Oh, yeah, he told me he gets butt raped every night."

"You hear that, dork?" and a punch to my arm.

"He hears it alright, but from the looks of him he'll probably like it."

I heard them but didn't really hear them at the same time. It was only nasty stuff that came out of their mouths. I'd be doing them a favor if I gave them

The Message

something nice and useful to say instead.

When Friday finally came around, I was feeling pretty excited. I reckon I'd been real bottled up and felt like I was going to get some relief and have something to look forward to. It was going to be a great weekend.

It was a long night. Mommy would have been proud. I found strength I never knew I had. Mr. Langley, in particular, was real heavy. I was lucky and got Josh and Amanda out on a date. Hunter was drinking which made him easier too. I was real glad our little old house was only one floor because I sure don't know if I would have been able to get them upstairs!

I felt a little bad about stealing them four long boards from the lumber yard, but I didn't have time to think of anything else, and I hardly had any money. What money I did have I used to fill up Uncle Darrel's tank. I figured that would make him happy.

I did use my baseball bat on two of them a little bit, but for the most part I owed my good luck to Mr. Philpot and the fact he hadn't cleaned them cupboards out for probably the 30 years he'd been a teacher. I had just been able to make out the letters on one of the old brown bottles; it said "chloroform". I read up on it and it was real good for putting folks to sleep. And sleepy they was!

Josh came to first but there wasn't much he could do about it, seeming as he was tied down on that big old board. I also had tape across his mouth, so whatever he was trying to say was just a bunch of mumbly nonsense. I waited until they all woke up good because I wanted them to have clear heads.

I knelt down in the middle in front of them and did my best to calm them down so they'd listen good. "I really need ya'll to concentrate now. None of you been very kind to me but I'm giving you a chance to make up for it and help me out."

I had to untape Hunter's mouth because I could tell he was fixin' to vomit. Once he emptied his tummy on the board and the floor he tried to holler, but I taped him back up quick. As soon as they all settled down a bit, I went down the row and put headphones on all of them. I admit I had to steal a couple of the pairs as well as Amanda's music player because I only had 3 computers capable of playing audio files. But thanks to my hobby, I had all the monitors I needed.

I didn't count on them closing their eyes shut, so I had to threaten them with some mean things if they didn't keep on looking straight ahead. I dabbed away Amanda's tears because I needed her to see good.

I didn't have much in the way of fancy software, so I had to use the stuff at school in the computer lab. It was kind of fun putting it all together. I felt like some kind of movie director or something. Anyway, I set each video to playing and made sure they kept watching. I even double checked that all the headphones were playing the right thing all nice and loud.

It was still dark and I lit some candles. Mommy liked candles. I don't know, maybe it was silly, but I thought it might help.

I checked Josh's stuff one more time after the sun had come up. It was all working good. The screen was flashing "I I I I I I" over and over and over and the others were working right too. His headphones were blaring me hollering "I I I I I I I" over and over too. I was right happy with myself.

I let it all go on for a few hours more and probably would have went even longer, but the phone started ringing, and then when I peered out the window, I spied a police car turning onto our road. I hurried real fast back into my room. I figured I didn't have much time.

I grabbed the big old heavy axe I took from my Uncle's shed. I heard a pounding on the door. I made my way down the line as fast I could. The screens were still flashing and the headphones were still blaring the four words until the very end.

I started with Josh. I raised the axe high in the air. I

The Message

concentrated on those words one at a time with all my might. I brought the axe down on to his neck, then Hunter, Mr. Langley, and finally, Amanda. I had burned them words into their heads the best I could, and with each swing I cried and screamed them out loud too,
"I"!
"MISS"!
"YOU"!
"MOMMY"!

The Message

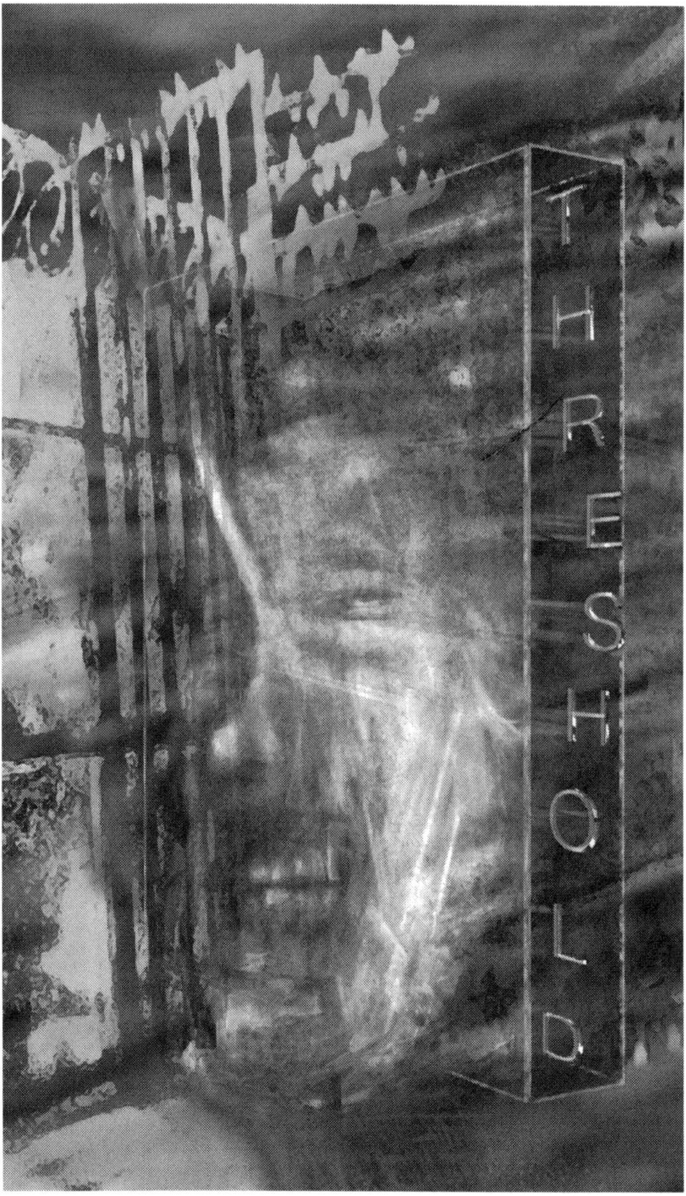
THRESHOLD

Threshold

Threshold

The turbulence of our times jolted me awake.

When I'm wide-awake in the cramped quarters of a plane, I like to pretend that I'm asleep and dreaming. I look around and imagine strange things happening - people floating out of their seats, stewardesses handing out tablets that make everyone hallucinate and laugh uncontrollably, or the pilot riding a go-cart down the aisle taking destination requests – anything to take my mind off the fact that I am a prisoner inside a stuffy, metal box.

I think that being in a plane crash – I mean in the process of one – wouldn't be so bad if I could sit at the controls at the time. I'd even settle for the co-pilot's chair just as long as I was able to white-knuckle the wheel and give a heroic tug backwards like you see in the movies. Instead of being back in coach shrieking like a little girl, I'd let out a fucking war cry with biceps bulging as I steadfastly try to gain control and defy what is most likely an inevitable catastrophe. Death wouldn't matter as long as I felt like I had some say in it up until the last second. Standard issue control freak stuff, I guess.

My head lolled to the left, and I cursed being forced into this stress position.

For the moment, a lovely, mocha-skinned stewardess was my main distraction. She was a vision potent enough to take my mind off the cramps. I love how they strap themselves in those seats against the wall and look back at you. Their glowing, reassuring faces like statues of the Blessed Virgin letting you know that, in the end, everything will be okay.

As I tried to rouse my sore body from its compromised state, she truly did appear to be an angel. Our eyes met and her smile was like a seductress, a favorite grade school teacher, and mommy all in one. I know that might sound a bit much, but I needed a savior of many forms to shepherd me through this ordeal. Then my eyes glazed over, and she seemed to disappear into the wall, and for a moment, I wasn't sure if she was there at all.

I realized I was already slipping into "game mode" and that my perceptions were not to be trusted, but this was a good thing. It's kind of like how the pilots rev the engines to make sure they're working just before accelerating down the runway. In my case, the less sure I am of what's going on around me and *inside me* the better. This is key to my success.

I've decided that we have landed and that I am supposed to rise and exit. I envision myself doing just that. I shake off the feeling that I've repeated this scenario a few times now. Even if I do get up, I'll spend a long time in a standing stress position before I begin the slow shuffle down the aisle with the others like a chain gang shackled at the ankles. Each act of de-planeing is like reaching for freedom all over again.

As I exited the plane, the intensity of the sun and the blistering South American heat just about brought reality crushing down on me. I cursed myself for this momentary show of weakness and performed my sensory flip-flop. What was momentarily painful was now a soothing warm glow. This was key to my survival.

I regained my concentration and headed inside the terminal that looked untouched since 1953. Every charming, retro detail was something to occupy my mind. The stone-faced customs officer broke into a wide grin showing off a magnificent gold tooth. "You will break", he said to me with relish.

"I'll break your fragile heart and take your month's wages if you bet against me", I replied and made a kissing gesture at him. Normally, I'd never be so flip to an official in a Third World country (or any country for that matter), but in this case, I knew he had no choice but to let it slide.

When I exited out into the main terminal, I was greeted with an explosion of madness – shouts, placards, curses, people jumping up and down waving their arms. I had never experienced anything like it. Back home this was all still underground stuff, but in this god-forsaken place it had damn near become a national sport.

Right when I thought the crowd was going to surround me and beat me to death, a couple big guys in uniforms grabbed me and hurried me off. I was shoved into a taxi and sent on my way.

The room was okay. I suppose I could have imagined better, but it was fit for purpose. I closed my eyes and soaked for a while in the tub and then opened my small, black, hinge-shut case with a silver skull on the lid. I selected one of the gleaming needles, took a deep breath and pushed it into the side of my wrist.

Bubble, bubble. Bubble encloses trouble. All the bumble bees are contained in the sphere. The nerves are merely the housing that connects the lenses. Me, the Scientist, looking, examining with clinical dispassion.

With as little forethought as possible, I rapidly stick a pin in a random part of my anatomy. The instrument of analysis swings around like a giant telescope in time lapse speed and captures the pain as if surveying an unremarkable galaxy in a distant quadrant of space. Ready for analysis and casual note taking, the victim does not exist.

We're all destined to meet the innards of a black

hole. And I see it. There I am, (remarkably calm for getting sucked into a singularity) glancing about, watching as every twinge of pain I've ever felt descends around me. A quiet, almost choreographed dance. The dance of descending and reduction. I see from up-close. I see from faraway. Vision and circumspection dilute pain. All things diminish under the withering stare of the detached.

I am a dog and pain is an odd noise in the brush. I merely cock my head, curious but unexcited. If I scream, it is just a howl at the moon.

I am a parched, sun-burned man in the desert taking a miraculously refreshing gulp of cool water just as a swarm of scorpions attacks my feet and ankles. I meet the sensation of exponentially tightening barbed wire with a flood of cool spring water.

My mind is a fireman. It can extinguish all fires of the flesh. I am my disembodied self observing my fleshy self right at the membrane of pain. From a third person point of view, it would appear that I have manifested a tougher double outside of me to spur me on like a harder older brother.

"C'mon bro, laugh it off!"

But what I have really done is to release the weaker me. It is the fragile me. The me containing all my frailties escapes. It stands and marvels at its mighty doppelganger for enduring such pain. And in return, the corporeal me basks in the glow of pride – the pride of being admired and overcoming the vulnerabilities of my sensitive side. I take the blows so that it can dream the stars. I don't want to let it down and that commitment reinforces my will to not so much overcome pain but to never let it get more than one foot in the door.

I don't much like the waiting. That's why I arrived late – only one night of struggling to sleep. It's a night that comes again and again.

I sat naked on the bed looking at my reflection in the mirror above the dresser. I reminded myself that tomorrow night I would be looking at the same body without a scratch in sight.

I put shorts on, and wandered out of my room. It was hot in the hall and it smelled of mildew. The wallpaper went well with the smell. I passed a few doors. One was cracked. I caught sight of a form standing in the room. It was The Buddha.

When our eyes met, I felt myself overcome by a strange, almost homo-erotic feeling, but on further consideration, it was more homo-sapien-empathetic...or something like that. I walked on.

A few meters down I turned into a nook where a soda machine, snack machine, and ice maker stood humming in a disharmonic symphony of companionship. I wondered if maybe the soda machine had a crush on the ice-maker and perhaps hated the snack machine for coming between them. Anything to keep my mind off the real world. I perused the selection.

"As for me, I feel at one with the m&ms"

I laughed before I even realized that it was The Buddha standing there saying it to me.

"I'd prefer a Xanax." As soon as I said it, I regretted it. I felt like I had shown a sign of weakness to him.

Mercifully, he let it pass and instead asked me how I felt about tomorrow.

"Crazy Ivan will crack. Orlando will cry like a fat boy teased at his first day of school. Otherwise, I guess that will leave me and you."

"And then?" the Buddha asked me as if he was truly waiting to hear what was sure to be the outcome.

"Then I transcend, shake your hand and the world disappears."

A pause and then a chuckle from the ever-stoic Buddha.

"And the Old Man?"

The Old Man...the Old Man. I had purposely left out the Old Man. I didn't know much about him. No one did. He intimidated me and I knew it. There's no denial in my world. It goes against my modus operandi. I had already decided my fear of him was going to be my weapon to defeat him. My lack of knowledge a force field to contain him. His secrets his weakness. I knew I was kicking around some mumbo-jumbo, but sometimes mumbo-jumbo can get your brain out of a tight spot.

"The old man will try to sit on the sidelines like a kid playing with a truck on the sidewalk alongside thundering traffic."

Now, I knew I was messing with The Buddha's head – throwing a kind of pre-game koan at him.

"But what will smash his toy?" The Buddha replied with sheer perfection.

"Fucker," I thought. He's too clever and that's why I knew it would come down to the three of us.

"Transcendence is an illusion – a balloon destined to be popped." The game was afoot.

"Balloon?" was all he said in reply.

I froze and searched frantically for a poker face. Instead I put coins into the machine and hit the button for m&ms. "Ka-chunk-chunk." The hatch made an alarmingly loud noise as I pushed my hand in to retrieve the snack.

I pulled the candy out and slapped the pack down into The Buddha's hand. "Be one with defeat".

"Oh, c'mon, you can do better than that," he retorted as I began to walk away.

"I will tomorrow," was the pithiest reply I could muster.

Back in my room, I prepared for a night of fitful sleep. I had been fiddling with the whole astral projection thing for a while, and this seemed like as good a place as any. The way I saw it, projecting out of your body was one thing but what if the body is in pain? What if you project into pure pain?

I managed to get a couple feet off the bed before I fell asleep.

"Clank. Scrape. Ka-chingle." The ice machine

pleads with the snack and sodas to stop fighting – to stop the madness. The teeth-scraping sound of rusty metal machine feet across brittle linoleum sounds like screams. Moving parts clash against other moving parts. Jagged edges everywhere. There is flesh in the fold. This form, this *Permutationist* tenses his radically exposed body and forces all sense and feeling up to the top of his brain where it radiates out like a gift to the cosmos. Encapsulated pain rises like bubbles. Watch them pass and marvel. At a time of your choosing, allow them to pop and release their awful potential back into the void.

I think I slept from 1am till 6. There was a light knock on the door. A shy and pretty woman handed a tray to me. Thick soup and bread with a large glass of milk. Right before the event I'll have some fruit and maybe a very cold milkshake if I can find one.

I hate the pre-game press conference, but it's all part of the hype. It makes the bookies happy as last-minute punters flood in. Who looks strong today? Who looks anxious?

They have us arranged in a semi-circle. As Crazy Ivan sits down, he obscenely sticks his tongue out at me and wags it like a sex maniac. One thing's for sure, with his bulging muscles, shaved head and numerous ghastly looking piercings, Ivan could undoubtedly kick all our asses in real life, unless maybe The Buddha was also like a secret Bruce Lee type or something.

I quickly looked away from Ivan and casually inspected my cuticles and let out an exaggerated yawn. As I have mentioned, I'm not particularly afraid of him. Deep down I think he's fragile. This is a game of depth and control, not brute force.

Orlando was, as always, dressed like a dandy. They had been sure to let enough locals into the medium sized room to squeal out his name and make a ruckus. The ladies loved him, but he was probably gay. Just as well, the Competition needs diversity. I heard there was a good female player up north somewhere, but I hadn't come across her yet. Apparently, she has kids and likes to bellow, "I have five huge kids. I've had bowling ball-sized heads come out of this!" as she crudely gestures down towards her crotch, "None of you scare me!" She sounds great. I hope we cross paths soon.

It seemed as though I was the only one who saw the Old Man silently enter the crowded room and glide otherwise unnoticed like a snake in high grass along the wall. He didn't so much sit as go from an upright position to a sitting one in a kind of slow motion.

Dueling English and Spanish boomed from the platform we all sat on. I understood none of it. "Tap, tap, tap." I played a tune on the table top with my fingertips. I glanced sideways and caught a flash of the Old Man tapping on the table as well, nearly in sequence with me. The deafening noise of the room sounded like one hundred radios playing at once. Despite the din, I felt like I could hear the Old Man's tapping. It was as if he was messaging me in Morse Code.

Perhaps he's suggesting an alliance. Maybe we can team up. I quickly chastised myself for thinking it. There was of course, strategy to consider, but now it felt like a sign of weakness.

This was a new game. There had recently been a leap forward in the technology - that was largely why this match was such a big deal. Now we all had the ability to dish it out as well as take it. I had only had a couple chances to mess with the new gear, and the official stuff probably functioned a bit differently. But this was suddenly very much a game of strategy.

Just when I thought I was about to decipher whatever cryptic message the Old Man was trying to send me, Ivan slammed his fists on the table and flew up knocking his chair violently over. He pounded his chest like Tarzan and made deep growling noises mixed in with Russian that I wagered even native speakers would struggle to make sense of.

Threshold

Having nothing against theatre, I decided to join the madness and leapt over the table. I approached a young woman, who appeared to be one of the reporter's assistants, and led her into a waltz of sorts. The crowd moved back just enough to give us room to sweep this way and that. Laughter and chatter mixed with Crazy Ivan's ravings. I glanced over at the Old Man. It was the first time I had ever seen a smile on his face.

I decided to stay out in the crowd as the various sponsors and officials said what they had to say. The reporters and other insiders then had the chance to ask us all a few questions. One tried to get the Old Man to say something, but he just stared. His round head with sparse, yet serious locks of grey hair streaming here and there didn't so much sit on his shoulders as hover there. I pictured it detaching and floating silently over to the person who had asked him a question and just hanging there an inch from their face. Breathing.

The topic of the new technology was the main line of questioning. No one knew what to expect. This was one of the first times it had been employed in an official match. I wasn't even convinced it would work, and besides, how could any of us be sure it was working even if it was? But I guess that was one reason I loved this game – the sheer uncertainty of it all. The way it was supposed to work is that we had to visualize our victim first or concentrate on the relevant, large number we all had to wear on our chests. Holding it in our heads, we were then to think hard on what torture we wanted inflicted. Needless to say, we had to do this while suffering whatever was being thrown at us. Psychologically, it was a massive change for most, if not all of us. I was still perfecting my system of pain exclusion/isolation/liberation and having to then also project concentration towards an outside entity was a major challenge.

Orlando stood surrounded by the adoring local press

Threshold

and habitually touched his perfect, jet-black air. Occasionally, his equally gorgeous female assistant would brush some imaginary dust off his shoulders. I liked him because it all seemed such a contradiction. He acted prim and a bit prissy, but I knew he could take punishment. He had outlasted several other South Americans who looked like they slept with vipers on beds of nails to earn the honor of participating in this event.

Once the circus subsided we all got led to small, separate rooms to get ready. Ivan and Orlando were the only ones who had a team with them. Me, Buddha and the Old Man preferred solitary.

The arena was an old cinema that had been hastily converted for the event. A semi-circular platform had been constructed by attaching risers that jutted out the front of the old stage at the sides. Then there was LED lighting on the floor demarcating a semi-circle. Large screens hung above us to provide close-ups as well as virtual simulations of what might be happening to us.

No doubt this would be a pretty boring competition to watch if it weren't for the audio-visual enhancements. It gave the crowd something to zero in on, to look for weakness, signs we were about to crack. Our faces often projected large to reveal anguish in minute detail. Gory effects thrown in to satisfy their blood lust.

I was on far stage left with Buddha beside me, then Crazy Ivan and Orlando with the Old Man at the other end of the semi-circle. It was a good position for me. In previous matches I could not have cared less, but this was a whole new game.

I staggered up onto the lucky horseshoe stage. I pretended like my right leg was killing me, and then I clutched my shoulder. An impatient official placed his hand on my back to urge me upward and I recoiled as if he had shoved a branding iron against me. The crowd howled with laughter and derision. Ivan jabbed a bulbous finger in my direction. I made the universal sign for "shrieking girl" as if tormented. Out of the corner of my eye I saw the Buddha doing his best to ignore me.

The converted old theatre still smelled of musty old curtains even though there was high tech looking machinery and bundles of wires about. Looming screens behind us displayed psychedelic images as techno music rumbled in the background.

We were allowed to take any position we wanted. I sank to my knees. I sat back on my heels and hung my head and began to contemplate the fuzzy interface between pain and pleasure. Like colored dye being added to water, I began to let all sensations merge.

I adjusted the metal bands around my ankles and wrists to make them as comfortable as possible. With the new tech they had to modify them a bit and they were slightly bulkier. I felt the first shock of an electrical surge speed through my body as the officials ensured that the system was transmitting efficiently. Impulses sent to ankles would register at the wrists and vice versa. A high tech band was wrapped around our heads for transmitting punishment at our opponents.

Enter the parade of torturers.

A grotesque coterie of evil filed out from a door in the back . The one wearing a gasmask with red, illuminated eyes raised his hands triumphantly in the air as the crowd booed and cheered. Then came Fatty – that disgusting flesh-bag of a human. Everyone knew he had no part in the wonderful intricacies of the science that underlies all this. He was just a filthy sadist plain and simple. It's a wonder he even knew how to use the system to deliver impulses. Someone must have coded a dum-dum interface for his sweaty, meaty fingers to pounce on to deliver whatever affront to human decency he threw at us. The system was designed to ensure that no one contestant received undue "attention". If Fatty threw too much pain my way, the system would begin to redirect it randomly at another competitor.

Helga came in last, fully decked-out in her neo-Nazi kit with a riding crop in her hand. The crowd loved her. Me, I wanted to stab her in the neck.

It had all become so show biz. Like a logical transition from "big time wraslin'" to virtual torture. Orlando and Ivan even had their small entourages and managers who played up the personalities of the two men. Preening over them and hurling insults at the audience and the cameras. Me, The Buddha and the Old Man were old school – just some fucked-up dudes out to push the boundaries of...Aaack! A lightning bolt of electricity shot through my body from my hands to my nutsack. Things were getting real.

I immediately look towards Ivan and concentrate harder than I ever have in my life and feel a cool satisfaction as I watch him fight in vain to keep his hand from going to his eye that, if as planned, was now swarming with a horde of needle legged spiders. I keep it up until the sensation of my fingernails being ripped off breaks my concentration. I stare at them to convince myself it is not actually happening.

Razor wire across my back. I close my eyes and turn it into the pale, lovely hand of a women scratching an itch down my shoulder blade. I visualize the red number 9 on Ivan and fill his mouth with razor blades. I glance over and see his face contorting while he also grasps at his stomach. I look at The Buddha and I somehow know that it is he who is filling Ivan's gut with scorpions.

For reasons unclear to me, I stare at the Old Man and imagine his wrinkly head being wiped with a cool, soft cloth. I see his eyes open in bemusement before he looks over at me. So, maybe comfort *can be* transmitted as well as pain. Whatever the case, it took my mind off the sensation of my skin being peeled off.

Electrocution. Flogging. Cutting. Unimaginable pain. I sit bolt-upright so I can look my body over to reinforce that none of it is truly happening, but I lurch forward anyway when I feel the bottom of my feet getting smacked hard. I isolate them in my head and picture them as fake, rubber feet from a joke shop being paddled by a child. I think I laugh. My laughs are swallowed by the sound of a wail. I twist my neck and it feels shackled. I glimpse The Buddha. He is near breaking point. It is very unsettling to see him in such a state. Through the red pain engulfing me, I see Ivan staring like a madman in Buddha's direction. I take all my pain and with a mighty heave, shove it at him. Crazy Ivan's face contorts and he reels back.

I don't even hear the horn blare. Finally, like a warm shower washing over me I feel the pain subside. Break. Intermission. Time for final betting as the crowd gets to look us over as we attempt to collect ourselves. None of us look in very good shape as we hobble off the stage and are led away. Once alone in a small, dark room I flex my muscles and run my hands over my skin. "I am a hard-ass. I am invincible. I can survive anything!"

I do my best to bolster my confidence, but even when the pain ceases there are after-effects. It may just be "virtual torture" but the nerves remain frayed and stressed. I close my eyes and run my hands all over my body to reinforce the knowledge that there are no wounds. Just as this exercise finishes I hear the siren. As I rise to exit the cell, I feel something sticky on my hand.

I have no time to examine it as I find myself back in the confusion of blaring lights, shouts and screams. I glance at The Buddha and he looks pretty bad. It dawns on me that maybe he isn't able to dish it out and is therefore getting the pointy end of the stick. I can't allow myself to feel sorry for him, but then I had already given the Old Man mental assistance. If I was going to survive this, I needed to get my shit together.

As soon as the horn blares, I throw everything I have at Ivan. I concentrate so hard on giving him pain that I begin to question my own humanity. Beside him, Orlando does his ridiculous dance as he attempts to turn the pain into bad disco. Every vein on Ivan seems ready to pop. Either the system or one of the players is punching me in the kidneys.

I see the Old Man glance at me and then he turns his head ever so slightly towards Ivan. Seconds later, Ivan crumbles. Beside me The Buddha cries out. Orlando's dance has become more like a seizure. I feel a punch to the face and then to the gut. I struggle to breathe. I see Ivan struggle to reach the button that will tap him out. He's done. But there's no button.

Orlando shrieks in a way that unnerves me. He collapses. I finally notice The Buddha on the ground beside me, writhing like a snake. More glare. More shouting. More pain. So much pain. I can take it. I can survive this. I use every trick in the book to convince myself that I am fine.

Ivan, Orlando and The Buddha are a mess. Something is wrong. Their agony does not abate even as they are begging it to stop. I look at the Old Man and try to give him a sign to throw in the towel. Instead of transmitting pain to him I attempt a message - that we should both give up at the same time, call it a draw. I can tell he is ready. But I can't. I can't give up. The pain becomes unbearable. I can no longer keep it in a bubble. I'm afraid I will smash my teeth from clenching them so hard. I look one last time to the Old Man. He is convulsing. I beg it to stop.

As I falter on the brink of blacking-out or worse, I finally get a look at my sticky hand. Crimson red. I know it is time for my last-ditch defense. I think of her, her lovely hair, her beautiful face, and that smile. I miss her so. And at last, as the warm glow of her presence fills my mind, the pain retreats even as my imagination fails me.

In my last moment, I know that we all have lost. These men, that I hardly knew, fought to remain alive as hard as I did. I can only hope that in the very end, they had a secret weapon too.

As all sensation leaves me, I triumph over pain and see her holding my hand at sunset and decide to declare it a victory even as I pray that she forgives me for not surviving.

Epilogue.

Shortly after dawn, on the 15th of September, troops overran a compound buried deep in the jungle. The facility had been hastily abandoned. Inside they found the remains of five captives. They are later identified as Ivan Solokov, a Russian embassy official, Orlando Marquez, a local human rights campaigner, missionary David Chan, Political Science professor Charles Oakley and Justin Amberly, a freelance journalist and young, aspiring writer.

Threshold

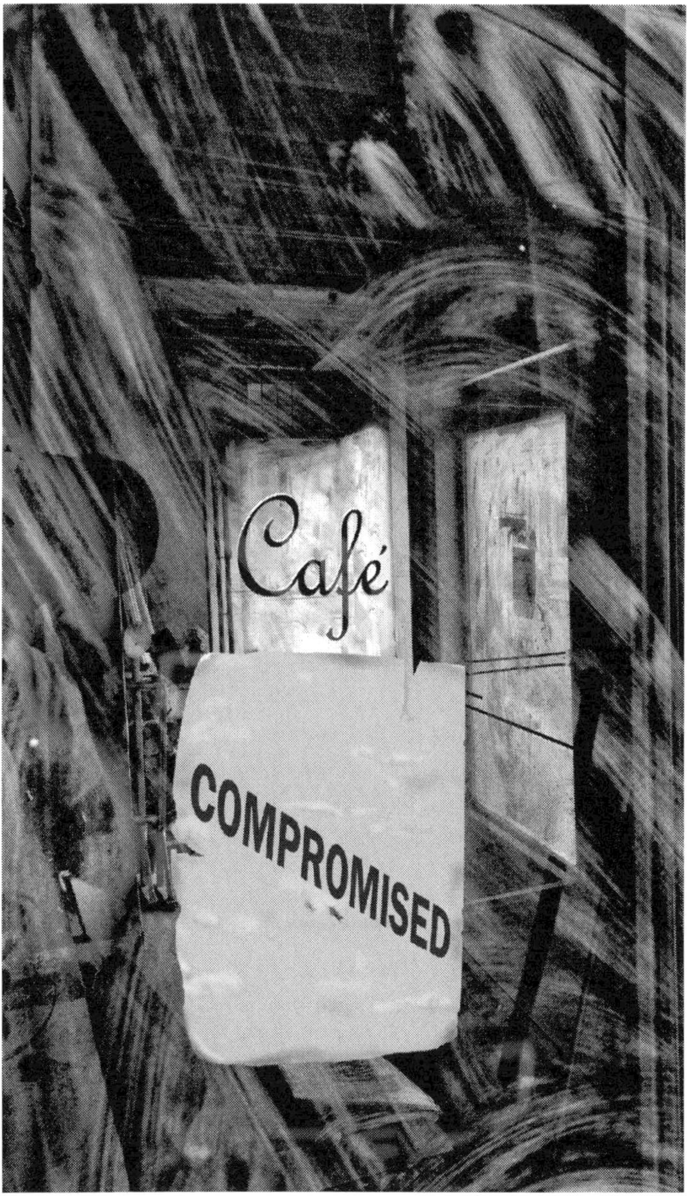
Café
COMPROMISED

Café Compromised

Café Compromised

I was relieved to see that my usual corner table in the "Cup of Tears" coffee shop was available. It was the one spot that allowed the most privacy whilst giving a sweeping view of both the other patrons as well as what was happening outdoors. On this day, I preferred to focus on the inside (both the inside of the café and what was in my head). If I could, I would seal off the outside and entomb these words forever within. Either way, I was very glad to have this table just now.

Flat white with a glass of water. I can't handle too much caffeine so I sip on the water to slow down. Even I can't justify being in there for 3 or 4 hours and only having one coffee. When it's time for the second one, I may order a decaf. It depends on who the barista is; if it's Julia, I'll have to go full caffeine and deal with the shakes and palpitations later. The café makes peculiar demands of the ego.

"Oh, gee, here he is," I mumble into my cup as I spy "Kurt" coming in. I only know the guy's name because of the barista calling it out when his cappuccino is ready. "'Cappuccino', what a joke! It's like the Pepsi Cola of coffee. Little baby need more bubbles in his coffee?"

I grimace as I watch out of the corner of my eyes as Kurt yet again cracks his knuckles and flexes out his hands whilst his laptop boots. It's the same bloody thing every time; the second the cursor appears, he acts like he's about to launch into the greatest paragraph ever written. I vow to go over later and get a peek at what app Kurt writes with. "Good god, I bet it's 'Word'. I bet he fucking writes with 'Word'. What a noob," I mumble to myself as I continue to be distracted by my extra-curricular narrative.

But this is one reason why we write in public (or what's left of it). Inventing characters and storylines in our head to commit to paper isn't always enough. With people around, one can more easily indulge in a complimentary narrative. The writer composing a story while "writing" about the others around him in his or her head gets double the relief. Add on to that, a tertiary narrative concerning this pillow-stacking of stories, and the writer reaches escape velocity. The princess creating a bulwark against the offending pea of the hideous real world. Narrative one – a thick skin. Narrative two – a bullet-proof vest. Narrative three – barricaded walls, and so on.

I try to get back to primary writing. I've been struggling with fleshing out a key confrontation between my protagonist "James" and the character's creative writing prof, who obviously doesn't understand the young prodigy's profound writing:

"If you were a decent writer yourself you wouldn't be here trying to crush the aspirations of young writers who are obviously more talented than you. In fact, you probably take out your frustrations on the best writer in every class, and in this case, it's me!"

I know the value of writing from one's own experience, and this indeed may have been one of those instances. It goes without saying that being a writer allows one to "say" things in writing that they wished they had said in person at certain points in time. Even if some great retort wasn't said at the time, the truth of it stands. "James" had vision. He had what a simple teacher of technique could never comprehend; he had imagination and depth.

"I can tell how much you envy one of my sentences by how hard you pressed down on the red pen when you struck it out. It must kill you to see a young guy like me write circles around you!"

I knew it would be the same with Kurt. In fact, I had started working on a character just like him - a guy named "Kirk" who enters a local short story competition and wins, even though the story is trite and hackneyed. One look at the judges and their "resumes" and it all makes sense. They are just the type who would go in for drivel like that. Kirk will get his photo taken at the award presentation, and it will get published in the paper. If, in the real world, I had submitted something, it would undoubtedly have rattled the judges and gone way over their heads.

I looked over at Kirk - Kurt, that is, and figured the same thing about him. He's probably writing about an Easter egg hunt where a murder happens and all the kids are suspects and it turns out in the end that they are all in on it but then the body disappears or some convoluted shit like that...wait a minute, that's not a bad idea. "Scribble scribble scribble".

Just then, Julia, the cute barista, goes over and starts to chat with Kurt. She motions towards his laptop. He turns it so she can see it. I watch as Kurt's face gets all serious as if he's trying desperately to explain the profound content of his writings. She strains to appear interested and nods her head.

"She's probably re-reading '*50 Shades*' trying to grasp the finer points," I scowl but then soften and decide that she's just humouring Kurt. If she ever asks me what I'm writing, I'll wave it off and instead ask her about herself and what she's up to. I'll show her that a guy can actually be interested in her life and not feel the need to prattle on about himself and his 'brilliant writing' all the time (though I'm sure my work would interest her more anyway).

The small bell attached to the top of the door goes "ding ding" as a new patron enters. "Oh, dear god, not a hipster," I groan as a bearded, be-spectacled guy with a man-bun strides in. Too-short, skinny jeans reveal sockless ankles. Out of breath from dodging the growing chaos outside, he manages a "Flat white, please." When Julia hands it over to him he studiously sips at it, pauses, then launches into some commentary on the quality of the bean. To the surprise of exactly no one, once he settles in, he takes out a laptop. Once open, it reveals a sticker on the back that reads "obey" next to a picture of one of the aliens from "They Live."

"Well, he certainly obeys the laws of fashions and trends," I think with a roll of my eyes. Let's see, he's probably writing about a young man fresh out of university who has decided to shake convention and wander the South West instead of getting a job. The guy, probably named "Trent" will encounter many weird and whacky characters along the way. He'll get into improbable situations, do some drugs and nearly get caught by some husband whose wife Trent is boning. It will be a wandering beatnik novel written by a guy who still lives with his parents.

This "Trent" will live a life on the road and one night, while tripping out on something powerful, will "discover" that the road itself is a sentient being that has its own agenda. Hold on, that idea's got legs! I quickly open my <ideas folder> and type out a quick outline. I've unwittingly given the hipster writer more credit than he's surely due. If he could read my mind right now he'd be frantically fleshing out that idea in order to beat me to the publishers. Even if he did beat me to it, the film made from his version would star somebody like Adam Sandler as "the voice of the road" and it would suck.

Thank goodness for the square business man

reading a paper by the window. At least there's one person to break up the cool factor in here. Oh, wait, what? He's getting a laptop out too? Surely, it's just spreadsheets or company email. I watch the man closely as he begins to type. Writing. He's fucking writing! It's the writer's pause that always gives it away. That's no email. Look at the way he loosens his tie, sighs and stares off into the distance, then writes. I already knew volumes about this guy. Trapped in a suffocating job, a dull marriage, this guy was trying to write his way out of his own reality. His halting prose most likely revolved around a shlub like himself, only his character leads a double life. He was bored at work and couldn't relate to his coworkers, especially the bosses. One night he had to go to a company function and overhears some shady talk not meant for his ears. He follows one of the bosses and discovers he and the company are involved in illegal dealings with foreign powers. Our office dweller becomes a most unlikely freelance detective. With each day, his life becomes more exciting and dangerous.

Before I could continue drawing the guy's entire life out, the café door opens again and a young woman walks in. Messy hair, Over-sized hoodie, piercing. Neo-hippie chick. She's a rebel this one. She orders a tea and best of all, instead of a laptop pulls out a well-worn notebook and begins to write. Is it a diary? A journal? Or is it a novel? A story about a young runaway named "Infinity" up against the patriarchy. Perhaps she meets a desperate young woman along the way. Her new acquaintance calls herself "Sunny". Sunny has resorted to sex work and recently she has noticed that a couple of the other street walkers have vanished. She is scared. She asks Infinity for help. But after that, Sunny herself disappears. The police aren't interested. Fatcat male politicians are somehow involved. Something evil is afoot.

No. She looks more like a poet. Plot-driven fiction would be too restrictive for this one. Neo-hippie chick is scribbling down her innermost feelings. Let's see. Something like...

I walk outside
My flat
At first the breeze
Feels good
But like all the rest
It changes
And tries to hold me back

Meanwhile, Kurt hovers over his laptop like a man possessed, as if he has 30 seconds to defuse a bomb (the bomb that his novel will be if he ever actually finishes it). He glances over at Hildegard the hippie chick hoping she is picking up on his intensity. Two fiery, creative spirits on the verge of a hook-up. It will end in arguments over one not taking the other's work seriously enough.

Just in time, the door springs open again. The commotion outside leaks in before she quickly shuts the door. A sense of relief as it's just an innocuous, middle-aged woman. Her carrier bag reveals her to be an everyday shopper out for a little retail therapy. One need not hear her order to know it's a "frappuccino-something". Thank goodness for a bit of the normal in here. One café can only accommodate so many literary rock stars.

Anyway, it's time to get some writing done myself. It's why I'm here after all. This little café a refuge from the taxing world beyond. A world from which there is no escape save the ramblings of the mind. I suppose one should not be so hard on fellow punters. Most likely they are only attempting the same, to find a bolthole in which to practice their craft. We who seek to be both in and out of this world...wait, what? Humdrum shopping lady has pulled a laptop out of her bags. Surely, it's just to check Pinterest or download coupons. But no, let me tell you, those of us keyed into such things *can just tell*. Those are the mannerisms of a writer. Again, the pauses, the flurry of typing, the staring off into space. Accuse me of stereotyping all you will, but that's got to be romance fiction she's writing. She probably self-publishes bodice-rippers on some web site catering to the wine and bonbon crowd. She sips her amaretto frappuccino whilst inventing impossible men and clever women. Star-crossed lovers having one more fling in exotic locales before it all comes crashing down.

I shouldn't be hard on her. Her kids are probably grown and completely self-interested. Her husband addicted to TV sports. Except we all know that such luxuries of the once predictable world are now in full retreat.

Sirens wail outside then go quiet. The few windows of the café obscured by mars and scars from outside. The door swings open again, and a nerd comes in. Yes, of course he's writing and yes, of course it has to be science fiction. Let's just pray it's not fan fiction of some sort. We'll give him the benefit of the doubt and instead posit that it's a near-future dystopia where brainiacs have been forced underground. Elites are hunted and the cult of ignorance rules. But then that sounds a bit too familiar to be sci-fi at this point.

Soon there is an elderly lady most definitely writing children's books and a school teacher working on young adult lit in the hopes of reaching increasingly feral youth with inspirational stories to help them make sound choices. A weird-beard squeezes in and dives right into some sort of philosophical literature where Nietzsche is a character living in Europe between wars. It's a very "meta" situation, because Nietzsche knows that everyone is holding their breath to see which way the wind blows when he gets a look at 1930's Germany. Will he or won't he? Double, triple agent Friedrich Nietzsche on the streets of Berlin circa 1932. Is it possible that some other shadowy figure encountered during some derring-do is none other than the "bearded one himself", Karl Marx?

I quickly scribble the idea down in the <ideas folder>. I'll be damned if I'll let post-modernism-Mike here claim that story. Soon I have to share my already cramped table with a very emo-looking young man wearing a torn, black jumper who hovers over his notebook Quasimodo-like. "Sanctuary!" I can hear his tortured soul cry as he pens a gut-wrenching tale of loneliness and darkness. His main character is most likely named "Anadijgan" or something like that. Anadijgan moves among the masses like a concrete-coloured ghost. Desperate for someone who is capable of comprehending him, he sets upon conversing with an old man under a bridge. He in turn sets the boy upon a journey to find the "Rune of Escape" so that he may transcend beyond the world of the normals.

The café fills to standing room only. Artists and drawers have crammed their way in as well. As I type, my elbow bumps repeatedly against a tall longhair rapidly, almost frenetically sketching a nearly abstract, windswept model. I half expect to see a chain reaction of one artist drawing another who is drawing and so on. *"The drawing of the drawer drawing a drawer"* will most likely never be seen as safe exit from the café grows increasingly unlikely.

It's so easy to make fun, to take the piss out of others whose work you will most likely never see, to play up the scorn, to bask in a hyped-up competitiveness that downplays the fact that you're all basically fighting for the same thing. But teamwork does not come naturally to the likes of us. If it does, it comes in the form of a few of us desperately trying to buttress a table top against the door or to tear off and nail the bathroom door over the windows as glass shatters.

Sirens wail then go silent. Sirens or screams. The smoke and mayhem press against the café. One of the creatives inside shouts out towards the end, "We are like the carbon of this tragic world crushed into a diamond! May our efforts somehow live on even as we are smothered and extinguished!"

We all ever-so-briefly turn flush with pride and mutual affection.

And somewhere along the line, as I and others type, scribble, write, draw, imagine and endeavour, the walls give way. What is outside cannot be over-written. In the end, creativity becomes our cyanide capsule. Are all our efforts in vain? In life, our work failed to stem the rotting tide. Now, all we can do is try to paint an exit and write ourselves out of this world, until this, our final stronghold, collapses and all things cease in mid-sentence.

Café Compromised

David Holtek is an artist who writes or a writer who draws. It must be one or the other. The Occupational Conservation Society has deemed it so. Some of his work can be seen at ArtVice.com. All story cover design by the writer.

"The paintbrush and the pen are the cowboys who corral ideas and images, the goatherds of the fantastic, the tools of the automatic trades. Paintings and drawings give a static glimpse, while stories can flesh out what might be running underneath. Write a painting. Draw a story. Mold this world of appearances to soften (or harden) the blow. These things may not be given as real, but reality summons them nonetheless. The textual frontier - the reach of the hand and horizon of the mind."

I have a few new stories in process and will eventually release another collection but next up will be my novel *Academic Investigator 5*. 'How will you know it's you when you appear?' Coming soon from Creative Disease. Thanks for reading.
David, October 2017.

Made in the USA
Columbia, SC
02 February 2019